A LION'S PRIDE

THE SERIES

When A Lioness Snarls

(A Lion's Pride, #5)

Eve Langlais

Copyright © March 2016, Eve Langlais
Cover Art by Yocla Designs © February 2016
Edited by Devin Govaere
Copy Edited by Amanda L. Pederick
Line Edited by Brieanna Roberston

Produced in Canada
Published by Eve Langlais
1606 Main Street, PO Box 151
Stittsville, Ontario, Canada, K2S1A3

http://www.EveLanglais.com

ISBN-13: 978-1530890019
ISBN-10: 1530890012

Chapter One

This is the life. Luna didn't care what anybody said. Nothing could compare to the enjoyment of sunbathing in a warm patch of sunlight while the chill of fall gripped the city outside.

She stretched on the fabric-covered pile of cushions, extending all of her limbs, practically purring in delight as the rays of brilliant sunshine streamed through the large plate-glass window of the condo.

"What the fuck are you doing?" The shocked male voice didn't startle her. Noisy wolf. She'd heard him coming for a while. He really needed to work on his stealth technique.

Exhibiting a laziness that usually only a male lion could achieve, Luna opened an eye and peered at the man standing, arms folded over his chest, across the room. He glared—how cute. "Hi, Jeoff."

"Don't you hi Jeoff me. What the hell are you doing in my apartment? Naked."

He'd noticed. Point. "I'm naked because it turns out you have a delightful afternoon spot, right about here." She indulged in a long stretch atop the cushions that she'd yanked off his couch and upon which she lay with her arms and legs extended. The pose pulled her tanned skin taut. Tanned with no lines, she should add. She'd recently gotten some time on a beach for a job in the south. It was a shifter-friendly locale and clothing optional.

"You do realize that the folks in the building across from here can see straight in."

How positively titillating. "Are they watching, do you think?" Luna rolled to her stomach and peered out the floor-to-ceiling glass window. She waved, but with the sun streaming in, couldn't tell if anyone watched and waved back.

A heavy sigh let her know Jeoff still stood behind her. As if she could miss his presence. Jeoff wasn't the kind of guy a girl could ignore. And not just because he reeked of dog. Dog as in a wolf shifter, not a true canine, although the two species did smell remarkably alike.

But she could forgive his furry fault because he was the standoffish hottie everyone wanted to bang. Like seriously, anyone with a pulse wanted to strip and ride Jeoff cowgirl style.

He had only himself to blame. Tall, much taller than her, Jeoff had broad shoulders but a lean build, an athletic build with defined muscle. He wasn't like the lions in her pride, all beefed up and impressed with himself. While a touch nerdy with his glasses and three-piece suit—the glasses a bit of a superhero accessory to his public persona—Jeoff was all man. And an uptight prude.

"If your naked ass ends up on the Internet, don't come yowling to me."

"I've got nothing to be ashamed of," she announced with a grin.

"Impossible," he muttered. "Just impossible to reason with."

"Don't blame me because you can't grasp the female mind."

"The female mind is easy compared to that of a lioness. You're all freaking nuts."

"Why thank you." Another sigh from him already? That might be a record, and another point.

"Why are you here?" Jeoff asked with an exasperation that had taken her under five minutes to achieve. The wolf proved such an easy mark to frazzle.

"I am here on pride business." Luna flipped to her feet and padded toward Jeoff, leaving her sunny spot behind.

Don't worry, my precious. I'll be back. The winter months were about to begin. She'd need all the sunny spots she could find for napping.

"Does your business always involve breaking and entering?" Jeoff asked as he turned from her and headed to his kitchen.

"Not always, but more often than you'd think."

He stuck his head around the fridge door to ask her, "Because the job demands it, or because a certain kitty got curious?"

"Jeoff, that is so species-ist. I should totally kick your ass for that."

He straightened out of the fridge and handed her a beer. "Kick my ass later. Get some clothes on and then you can tell me what kind of business brings you here."

"I don't need clothes to talk."

"Maybe you don't, but I refuse to listen while your coochie is hanging out."

Some people could be such prudes. "I'll have you know my coochie does not hang because I do Kegels daily." Luna did a squat just to see him avert his eyes to the ceiling.

But he wasn't completely uninterested. The bulge in his pants was too pronounced for that.

Well, well. Maybe Jeoff isn't as immune as I thought. And she really did wonder. She'd had her eye on the wolf for a while now, had even made a few overtures that he'd politely brushed aside. According to him, he dated only human girls because, "They cause less drama."

Kind of boring really. But hey, his loss.

"Put some clothes on. Now." Funny how a single guy in his early thirties could totally channel the voice and tone of a father.

Luna wasn't a little girl, though. It didn't take much to pounce him from behind and wrap naked limbs around him. She yelled, "A naked woman is touching you!" She totally couldn't wait for him to freak out.

What she didn't expect was to get flipped onto her back on the cushion-bereft couch with him poised atop her.

His eyes practically blazed. "Are you demented?"

She smiled. "Only when I take after my mother's side."

"And what did you inherit from your father's side?"

"Ability to burp the alphabet in one shot."

"That is not something I'd brag about to people."

"That's what my Aunt Zelda keeps telling me. Says my grandmother is probably rolling over in her grave. Which I see as a good thing. I'm sure she wants to stay in shape in case the zombie apocalypse comes and she needs to chase down brains for dinner."

"I should know better than to try and have a conversation with a cat. You're all impossible." He rolled off her and got to his feet. Moving a few feet, he dropped onto a chair that retained its cushion. With his free hand, he yanked at his tie and loosened it.

"Tell me why you're here and then go."

"Aren't you going to beg me to put some clothes on?" Luna perched on the couch across from him, legs primly crossed, hands on her knees, shoulders back. The picture of perfect posture.

He kept his gaze trained on her face. "Naked looks good on you. So, no, you can stay that way. I'm good."

Oh. Point for him since he'd managed to surprise her, and dammit, he knew it judging by the twinkle in his eye and the deadly dimple in his cheek.

"Are you flirting with me?" Shyness wasn't something Luna suffered from.

"I don't date—"

"—shifters, and especially lionesses. I know." She rolled her eyes. "I still don't see why. We could have so much fun. No strings. Just hot, sweaty sex for hours and hours."

"If it takes him hours to get you off, then he's not doing it right." For a moment, his eyes flared with fire.

"Don't tell me you're a two-minute wonder."

"Whatever helps you not lust after me at night."

"I don't lust after you."

"Says the woman sitting naked in my apartment. I know a dating service if you're that hard up."

At the implication Luna couldn't get a man, annoyance burned. She leaned over and grabbed her T-shirt from the armrest it had landed on when she'd stripped earlier. Tugging it on, she noted his gaze a little south of her neckline once her head popped through the hole. She hid an inner smirk as she smoothed the fabric over her frame.

He might push her away, yet he wasn't unaffected.

Just playing hard to get.

She could dig that, although she would admit she didn't usually flirt with a man so blatantly. Luna preferred a more forthright manner. Usually of, "Hey, you're hot. Wanna check out my ceiling?"

Her ceiling, his ceiling, either worked so long as he didn't have a ceiling fan. Watching them spin made her dizzy.

"Check it out, Captain Prude. I am wearing clothes. Are you happy now?"

"Not particularly. Have you seen what's on your shirt?"

She peered down and grinned. The shirt displayed a buck-toothed beaver, wearing lipstick, with the stamped words, *Pet My Beaver*. "Isn't it cute?"

"I don't recall the last beaver I saw being that hairy." Utterly deadpan.

Yup, he'd totally noticed the trimming down south. "Want to pet it?"

Again, he went still, his eyes flashing with a wildness there one second, gone the next. "Enough with the verbal games. Let's get down to business. Why are you here?"

"Word has it you're looking for some missing wolves."

"No idea what you're talking about. The pack is perfectly fine." As the alpha dude in charge of the small group of city wolves, Jeoff would know. And apparently, Jeoff lied.

Luna blew a raspberry. "Bullshit. You've got unexplained disappearances, and the way I hear it, the ones you are looking for aren't the first ones to go missing. It's not just your pack with that problem."

Brow creased in a frown, Jeoff asked, "How do you know about the missing people? I haven't released that information to anyone."

She shrugged. "The pride has its ways." She wiggled her brows and grinned.

Their ways consisted of Brody's new girlfriend, who happened to be Jeoff's sister, keeping them well informed of what happened in the small city pack.

"I still don't understand why you're here. The people who have gone missing are wolves, which makes it pack business."

"A pack that abides by pride rules." When predatory groups shared living space within an area, one always took dominance. In this case, the lion's pride ruled, with Arik, their fearless leader, at the helm—and the lionesses to act as muscle.

"No rules have been broken. There is nothing to report. We have no evidence of foul play. No clue at all as to why they're gone. I don't see why the pride would get involved."

"Because we've had people go missing too."

Chapter Two

"What do you mean some of the pride have gone missing?" Jeoff asked the question, yet what he really wanted to say was, *"Take off that shirt."* Because, while he might have demanded Luna get dressed, in truth, he truly preferred her naked.

As he sat across from her, it was all Jeoff could do not to leap across the space between them. From the moment he'd walked into his condo and smelled that unique blend that was all hers—all woman—he'd felt an urge to act in a most inappropriate fashion.

Lick her up and down.

No licking. Not of this woman. Especially not this woman.

Jeoff had a firm stance when it came to not dating anyone from the pride, although the ladies— some not so ladylike—kept trying. It wasn't that the lionesses weren't attractive. They were gorgeous and lively and outspoken. They also came with drama and a family dynamic that put the pack one to shame.

Being with a lioness was agreeing to never having a private life or moment again.

Jeoff didn't think he could handle that. Just like he didn't think he could handle the smart-mouthed woman before him, a woman who didn't bow to anyone, except the pride's lion king, Arik. And even that was iffy at times.

He realized she'd been talking while he mulled,

and he caught only the last word of her speech.

"No tail?" He repeated it with a query.

She rolled her eyes and sighed. "Were you not paying attention at all?"

"No."

"You should have been born a lion," she snickered. "I said that we had a visiting couple from another pride go missing a month ago."

"How am I just hearing about this?" Part of Jeoff's duties for the pride was to provide security. He led the firm that employed humans and wolves as private investigators and bodyguards.

"Because we just found out. We all thought they'd continued their road trip and gone back home. Except last week, the missing woman's sister called us looking for her. Turns out no one's seen them since they checked out of their hotel here."

Which sounded eerily like his own case. Missing wolf couple, apartment cleared, no signs of foul play, but also no notice or message as to their whereabouts. "Is that the only case?"

Luna shook her head, sending her sloppy ponytail swinging. "Out in the suburbs, a recently married tiger couple also vanished. Same shit. House cleared out. Bank accounts wiped. It's like they never existed."

"I take it you haven't gone to the cops?"

The look she shot him, disdain with a hint of mockery, answered that question.

"So it looks like we have a common denominator in the disappearances. I still don't get why you're here. You obviously don't need information." Hell, he should probably grill her for information, as she seemed to know quite a bit.

Pin her to the floor and make her talk.

Somehow, he doubted shoving a certain body part in her mouth as incentive would help her speak. Unless he could decipher mumbles.

"The boss wants me to work with you." Boss being Arik. "He seems to think you're some kind of expert when it comes to tracking." An eloquent roll of her eyes showed what she thought of that. The lionesses were great hunters and weren't keen on help.

"I've been discreetly enquiring, but, so far, haven't come up with much. The neighbors never saw or heard anything." And he couldn't find any clues, mostly because a flood in the apartment above that collapsed the ceiling and made any kind of scent tracking impossible.

"The neighbors didn't notice a moving truck and guys toting all the shit away?" Luna's brow arched.

"Oh, they noticed, but didn't think anything of it. People move in and out all the time."

"So where did the shit go?"

He shrugged. "No idea. I ran a search on the moving company. One of the fellows in the building remarked on the name, Starting Over Moving Inc., but I haven't been able to locate them. It's part of the reason why I'm beginning to suspect foul play." While Jeoff didn't require pack members to advise him of their every move, common courtesy dictated that they'd let him know if they were planning to leave. But the fact that everyone was surprised by their disappearance, boss and friends alike, as well as family, plus the less-than-casual wipe of their existence, made Jeoff believe something had happened to that couple. Something bad.

"That's the same company that moved those tigers. So, obviously, we are dealing with some kind of conspiracy. I say we crush it." She slammed her fist into the palm of the other hand.

"Great plan except, first, we have to find whoever is responsible."

"Any suspects?"

He shook his head and took another sip of his beer before answering. "Nothing. As far as I can tell, they had no enemies. No one seemed to suspect they were anything less than human. They were well liked."

"What about hobbies? My missing pair doesn't seem to have anything in common other than the fact they were young. The ones missing from the hotel were both lions. Fit, blond, and fairly well off. Folks at the hotel where they were staying said they seemed very lovey-dovey. But who is to say the guy didn't snap a gasket and kill her before wiping all traces of himself and disappearing with their money?"

For a moment, he stared at her. "Do you think that actually might have happened?"

"It's possible, but not what I think happened. I met the dude. If anything happened, she killed him and hid his body. Dude was a bit of a pussy."

"Well, he was a lion. I'm sure he couldn't help himself." He held in a snicker.

She couldn't help a rueful smile. "There was a reason Lionel wasn't a contender for any positions in his pride. So I doubt he masterminded the disappearance. As for Kammie"—she shrugged—"I only met her once. She looked normal to me."

"Which, given who you hang out with, isn't exactly an endorsement."

"Are you dissing my friends?" A hot glare lasered his way. "Be very careful, wolf. You never know what I'll do to your kibble if you get on my bad side."

"You mean this, so far, is being on your good

side?" he razzed her, intentionally poking the alert lioness.

She smiled. "Couldn't you tell? No cops or blood yet."

"Speaking of blood, I need to eat."

"Eat? But it's only like five o'clock." Luna's nose wrinkled. "It's barely past lunch."

"If you're an owl." Unlike some of the more nocturnal species, Jeoff tended to keep a very daytime schedule. Up at six for a run. At work by eight, lunch by noon, and dinner around five. He didn't need his tummy to remind him of that fact.

"Why don't you get changed into something comfortable while I cook us up some shit to eat."

"Don't you dare go into that kitchen." Yes, he threatened. He'd heard of Luna's culinary ability second hand, usually accompanied by gagging gestures and choking sounds.

"Are you going to cook for me? I'm not really hungry yet, but I'm sure I can make myself eat if we go into the bedroom." Forget any kind of pretense. Luna boldly propositioned.

"We are not having sex, nor am I getting changed. I'm perfectly fine in my clothes. And since you can't seem to get to the point, I'm going to make myself a sandwich while you eventually get to the reason of your visit."

"I thought we'd ascertained we were working on the same case. Isn't that reason enough?"

"You could have called. Emailed. Texted. Done any number of things instead of coming halfway across town to harass me in person."

"Didn't anyone ever teach you that stalking is best done in person?"

The wink and sly tilt of her lips almost made

him drop the eggs.

Be afraid, be very afraid. A lioness has us in her sights.

And, no, he wasn't going to roll over and ask her to tickle his belly with her claws.

He wanted to feel those on his back!

Chapter Three

The look on his face as she told him she stalked proved highly entertaining. But the smoldering gaze that came after truly intrigued. He ducked into the fridge, hiding his expression, and spoke to her from within the cold, stainless-steel wonder—now sporting a perfect handprint that would scream to all who entered, Luna was here.

We should totally put a mark like that on the wolf too.

Her damned inner feline really seemed to have a thing for the canine. The forbidden treat—and one that kept resisting. Didn't he know the challenge only made her curiosity and determination fiercer?

"So you wanted to stalk me in person. Kind of desperate, but I guess if you get too frisky, I could get the spray bottle out and give you a squirt."

He totally deserved the foot she aimed at his ass. What she didn't expect was for him to whirl away from the fridge, grab her foot, and hold it upraised. She crossed her arms as if there wasn't anything odd at all with her standing on one leg wearing only a T-shirt. A T-shirt that didn't drop low enough to cover everything.

He noticed. The effort he made to be a gentleman proved interesting, his gaze struggling to remain on her face.

"Can't you behave?" he asked.

"No."

"I demand you at least refrain from kicking."

"Squirt me and I'll do worse than give you a boot."

A wicked grin stretched his lips, and it totally made her erotic engine hum. "No squirting? And here I thought that was the whole point of your flirting."

How dare he turn it into a sexual innuendo? She should have thought of it first. "And you think I'm hard to understand? Remember this moment later when we're both naked in the woods and I make a point of laughing and pointing at you."

Dropping her foot, he turned away and again rummaged in the fridge, emerging this time with several sealed containers, a package of cheese, a tomato, lettuce, and some mayonnaise. "Would there be any point in asking why exactly we're both going to be naked in the woods?"

"Because we're going to check the tigers' place out in suburbia."

"I thought you said it was empty."

"It is, but given the scene is still rather fresh, I want you to check it out, you know, put that nose of yours to use."

"I don't have to be naked for that."

"Well then, your wolf is going to look mighty funny when you're running through the woods in your tightie-whities."

He finished slapping his sandwich together. "You know, it's times like these that I remember why I hate dealing with lions."

"And yet you stay inside the city and continue working for us."

"Apparently, I'm a masochist." He took a bite of his sandwich and groaned.

Hell, she wanted to groan too. The thing was a

work of art. A towering beauty set on a crusty Panini bun. She'd watch him build it as they talked, making it look so easy—and delicious. Slathered with butter then lightly toasted on a hot press, the bread crisping as he sliced thin pieces of roast beef, which he then layered on the sandwich with cold bacon slices and dribbles of beef drippings. He also added some cheese on top before placing it back in the hot press. When the cheese bubbled, he slapped it onto a plate, dabbed some fragrant basil mayonnaise on top of the stack, two slices of tomato, some lettuce, and, *voilà*, a sandwich fit to steal.

Which she did, and immediately took a bite. "Mmm. That is damned good."

She'd lost count of how many sighs he'd uttered, but he upped the count considerably as he slapped together, in between hot glares, a second sandwich.

When it was finished, he stayed well out of reach. He was safe. The one she'd stolen had hit the spot.

She hopped onto the counter, almost wincing as her bare ass hit the cold granite. "Now that our bellies are full, ready to go on an adventure?"

"I don't suppose there's a second option?"

"Don't be a princess. This will be fun. Unless you really are teeny-weeny, then it might be a little embarrassing for both of us."

"The only thing small about me is my patience right now," he grumbled. "Let's go and get this over with. The sooner we do it, the sooner I can get home and relax."

"Trust me, wolfie, I'd rather be hanging with my girls, drinking tequila and playing darts."

"I thought the bar banned you guys."

"They did. Spoilsports. It's not like we took out anyone's eye." The human had only himself to blame. Grabbing Reba's ass like that. He totally deserved what he got.

"Give me a minute to change into something a little more practical." He left the kitchen, and seconds later, a door slammed shut, someone apparently looking for some privacy.

We should go take a peek. Because it would totally make him snap, and for some reason, she enjoyed doing that. Despite Luna having known Jeoff for years, this was probably the longest she'd ever talked to him one-on-one. The more he rebuffed her, the hotter he got.

Given he was uber hot before, he was supernova now. Didn't he know that playing hard to get was a turn-on?

When he emerged from the bedroom, he was not wearing his glasses. A shame, she kind of liked them. Without them, his eyes proved piercing. Dark green, the green of a forest at twilight. Before, when Jeoff wore his suit, she was only given a general impression of his shape, but in his form-fitting black T-shirt, she was treated to his lean build, nicely toned and defined. A man who was fit, but not bulky.

His shirt clung to his torso and hung over the waistband of his athletic pants, the kind with discreet snaps at the side for easy ripping.

"You going barefoot?" she asked with a peek at his large—yes, *large*—feet.

"You going bare-assed?"

"I guess I should put my pants on for the ride over." Her turn to utter an exasperated sigh, as if put out by his suggestion. In a sense, she was. Guys didn't usually tell her to put her pants on. Her Aunt Zelda, though? *If you're going to do cartwheels, wear some damned underwear!*

She slid on her pants and pulled on her jacket while he slipped his feet into running shoes and grabbed a coat of his own. When he would have grabbed keys, she shook her head. "I brought my wheels."

What she didn't mention was there were only two of them, something he didn't seem too keen on.

"No way." Jeoff shook his head once they stood outside by the street curb.

Already straddling the motorcycle, Luna slid forward as she fitted her goggles over her head, her only concession to safety—because she hated catching a bug in the eye. "Get on. There's plenty of room."

"I am not riding bitch on your bike."

"Is this some macho thing?" She started the bike, letting the deep rumble fill the air before adding, "Are you emasculated at the thought of the enjoyment I'll have hugging this steel beast between my legs?"

"No, I'm wondering if my medical insurance will cover the hospital visit for the road rash I'll probably get if I let you drive."

"I will have you know I have a purrrr-fect driving record. As if I'd let my baby hit the ground." She rubbed the tank on her bike, the bright pink flames probably the most girly thing she owned.

"Can't I call a cab instead?"

"Sure. I mean, I'm sure no one's going to start any rumors about the head of the local pack being too yellow-bellied to get on a bike." Ooh, she didn't get a sigh that time but an actual growl. He swung his leg over the ass end of the bike, and she couldn't help but remark, "I have to say, wolfie, the heat of your glare is just making me warm all over." Which she needed.

While there wasn't any snow on the ground, the air was chill. Very chill. But he was hot, oh so very hot, especially when he fit himself to her backside and wrapped an arm around her waist.

"Drive."

The huskily whispered words sent a shiver through her. Perhaps she gunned her bike a little much. It shot off, but Jeoff held on—unlike her last short-lived boyfriend. He'd let a flesh wound get in the way of sex. Pussy. Needless to say, it didn't work out.

Weaving in and out of traffic, she couldn't help a small thrill as Jeoff's body moved with hers, dipping and leaning as they took sharp corners and made good time through the gridlock—and not one person screamed she was a crazy bitch. Surely a record.

Within less than thirty minutes, she pulled into the driveway of the vacant house that, just over a week ago, hosted a happy tiger couple in love. Now it sat empty and dark.

She shut off the engine. In the stillness, the only sound marring the silence was the hot ticking of metal cooling. A glance at the house was all it took for a shiver to run through her. Usually, she didn't let shit bother her; violence was a fact of life. But this… This systematic erasure of two people, the complete and utterly thorough fashion in which their lives had been wiped, freaked her out.

Jeoff didn't move, his arms still around her. "Cold?"

She shook her head. "No." But she wasn't about to explain her trepidation. He'd mock her for sure and with good reason. She wanted to mock herself. This was just a house. Nothing more.

"How are we getting inside?"

"I've got the key." She had to leave the warm

cocoon of his body so she could stand and dig it out of her pocket. She held the single gleaming key up from the little ring.

Most men would have snatched it—feline ones at any rate. You couldn't dangle anything in front of them without them taking a bat. Jeoff didn't grab it, though. He got off the bike and went to the front door, head cocked at an angle. With the tips of his fingers, he pushed it open.

"What the hell? Someone forgot to lock the place. Arik will be pissed." The pride owned this property and many others like it, renting them to shifters at better-than-market rates. Their way of helping out those just starting out and who wanted something other than condo living.

"It wasn't an accident. Someone kicked it in." He pointed to the cracked frame. He dropped to his haunches, and she noted his nostrils flaring as he breathed in. "Only one scent."

"Human?"

"Maybe. Whoever it was wore a heavy cologne." He bent lower and sniffed the front stoop, hands flat on the concrete. "They also wore running shoes, fairly new ones." Getting to his feet, he dusted his hands off on his pants. "Shall we?" Shoving the door open, he stepped in first. Jerk. He was totally trying to act the hero and get first dibs at the fun.

She quickly joined him inside the house. They both paused in the front hall. A pungent aroma filled the air.

"Is that…" Her nose wrinkled. "Pee?"

"Pee and something else," he murmured, poking his head into the dark living room, the carpet a sponge for whoever had broken in.

"Bloody vandals. We're going to have to call in

some floor guys and get this stripped and replaced."

But Jeoff wasn't listening to her being practical. He stepped into the improvised bathroom and took a deep inhalation.

"Whoever did this enjoyed some asparagus beforehand," Jeoff mused aloud. "The aroma is quite distinct when expelled in urine."

"So what if they ate asparagus? Why does that matter?"

"Because it was quite possibly intentional. It is one of the foods a person can ingest to camouflage their true nature."

"And you know this because?"

"I handle security. Sometimes hiding in plain sight can be useful. And asparagus is a lot more palatable than say spraying myself down with toxic perfume."

"Scent camouflage is crooked," she grumbled. "I never hide who I am."

"That's because discretion isn't a word you recognize."

Oh, she knew all about discretion. She just chose not to employ it. Luna was all about the truth—even if it hurt.

Jeoff moved from the smelly living room farther into the house, poking his head through a door to peek at the main floor bath. He paused for a moment in the empty den—the office, and not bear-cave kind. At the back of the house they found more chaos.

Hands planted on her hips, Luna shook her head as she noted the cupboards, the doors all open, some hanging askew, a few torn from the hinges and littering the floor. More reno work. Arik wouldn't be happy, but then again, who could have predicted this kind of pointless vandalism? It wasn't as if anyone other than a select few knew the house was empty. It had been only a few days since the couple vanished.

The smell of urine wasn't as strong in the kitchen, especially once she opened the basement door and a noxious gas cloud wafted out. "Smells like a demon farted down here," she remarked.

"Fuck! That's rotten eggs, which means there's a gas leak. Get outside." He moved to the sliding glass door and fumbled a second with the lock before he yanked it open.

The sudden influx of fresh air had her moving toward him, eager for a gulp.

From the back end of the yard, something bright came spinning out of the darkness, headed right at them.

"Move!" Jeoff yelled, grabbing a hold of her and practically throwing her outside. As glass broke with a distinctive tinkle, she had a moment to think, *That can't be good* before a fist of hot air hit her in the back and punched her.

Chapter Four

The force of the explosion lifted Jeoff from his feet and sent him flying. He knew enough to tuck, so he hit the ground partially protected and immediately rolled to his feet.

While the wolf in him immediately wanted to chase after whoever had flung the Molotov cocktail, his first concern was Luna.

Apparently, he wasn't on her list, though. A snarl ripped through the air, and before he had time to pivot, he noted her golden shape bounding off into the woods. She'd managed to shrug off her coat, but her jeans and shirt were a write-off. Still, he grabbed her shit and ran for the edge of the woods, dropping them in a pile just out of sight of the house, which billowed smoke and lit the dark yard with the orange glow of hungry flames.

He quickly shed his own garments, dropping them on top of hers, urgency firing him. His wolf demanded they go on a hunt, and they would, but the man-half was also practical. They couldn't exactly go home in the buff.

Naked, he crouched and called forth his beast. Not that it truly needed urging. The animal half of his psyche was never far beneath the surface.

Skin rippled, fur sprouted, limbs twisted and contorted with a pain that would send a regular human into a catatonic state. But he was strong. Fierce.

Wolf…

As his four paws hit the ground, his head lifted and he howled, an eerie ululation that announced, "I'm on the hunt."

He didn't need to press his nose to the ground to find a trail. Everything was so clear to him in this shape. Odor practically had a color and shape, the various threads of it visible and easy to follow. While a part of him longed to chase the cat—and perhaps corner it in a tree—he stuck to the discordant flavor in the air, the one that smelled out of place. The same cologne he'd smelled on the front porch.

Fleet of foot in this four-legged shape, he bounded through the forest, the protected parkland stretching acres in all directions, so many places for prey to hide.

In the distance, he could hear the approaching scream of sirens, firefighters on their way to save a hopelessly lost house. Closer, he could hear the crunch as his paws hit the fallen foliage layering the ground. The scattered leaves swirled and rustled, marking his path.

But he wasn't looking to hide. He was on a hunt.

Whoever he chased proved fleet. Jeoff was fast, but not fast enough, and neither was the lioness. He caught up to Luna at the edge of a road bisecting the forest, pacing the gravel shoulder, the lingering scent of car exhaust still in the air.

It was where the trail ended. Their prey had escaped.

She morphed out of her lion and paced in the flesh. Very nice naked flesh. "Fuck!" She repeated the word a few times as she strutted back and forth in agitation.

He lay down, head on his paws, and listened to her rant.

"I can't believe he outran me. And on two feet! That's like unheard of. He mustn't be human. No human could beat me in a foot race."

She had a point. But if it wasn't human, and it didn't smell like shifter, what did that leave? Jeoff had never heard of anything with two feet being able to outrun a wolf and lioness.

"And what was wrong with his scent? That cologne was rudely overpowering. You'd think he doused himself in it."

Which begged the question, why? What had the arsonist wanted to hide?

"What I'd like to know is why the hell he torched the house and tried to barbecue us with it. Was he afraid we'd find a clue?"

If the arsonist had left something behind, then they'd missed it. Whatever it was would turn to ash, leaving the case of the missing tigers shrouded in mystery.

She turned her irate gaze on him, five-foot-almost-nothing of blonde irritation. Cute as hell, if deadly. "And why hell are you still in your doggy shape? Is it because you're afraid I'm going to point and laugh?"

Was she on that again? Time to put her conjecture to rest.

He switched shapes, the reverse process no more pleasant. What he did find fun was the widening of her eyes as she let herself stare unabashedly at his groin.

"Damn. Do you, like, pass out when that thing gets hard?"

Chapter Five

It was hard to not giggle as Jeoff, his back ramrod straight, stalked back toward the burning house, bare feet stomping the leaves.

"Oh come on. It was a legitimate question. I mean, you only have so much blood to spare, and that thing is massive."

"I don't pass out," was his terse reply.

"Do you just moan and grunt like Frankenstein?"

"My speech is perfectly fine during sex."

"Really? I mean, you'll have to excuse my skepticism. After all, I am taking only your word for it. Feel free to prove it. I'll sacrifice my virtue for the greater good."

"Virtue?" He snorted.

"Hey, are you implying something?"

"Boldly stating. We both know you're far from a virgin."

"Nothing wrong with a lusty appetite," she grumbled, but she couldn't stay mad with the most perfect ass flexing in front of her. "So, what's the plan when we get to the house? Find some marshmallows? Ooh, maybe a hot fireman. They smell delicious. All smoky and—"

Before she could complete that thought, she found herself caught against a naked body and propelled against a nearby tree trunk. Green eyes, bright and wild, glared down at her.

"Do you ever stop?" Jeoff asked.

"Stop what?"

"Talking."

"If you've got a problem with it, then make me stop. We both know you've got the right tool for it." She couldn't help an impish grin.

"How many times do I have to say it's never going to happen? I don't get involved with lionesses. I doubt my sanity or insurance could handle it."

For some reason, his adamant stance bothered her. "You say that, and yet you've never even given us a chance." Never given her a chance, and this despite the fact that Luna knew he found her attractive. Just ask the erection trying to poke her.

"I don't have to give you a chance because I know the outcome."

"Do you?" Despite his constant rebuffs, she couldn't help trailing the tips of her fingers down his bare ribcage.

He sucked in a breath, and his eyes shuttered halfway, but even that couldn't hide the glow. The pattering of his heart stepped up a notch. He dipped his head and whispered, "We have company."

Whirling away from her, he dropped into a half-crouch, ready to defend her. How cute.

But unnecessary. She sighed. "Your timing sucks, Reba."

From between the tree trunks stepped her mocha-skinned friend. She dangled Luna's leather jacket from one hand and had the rest of their clothes tucked under her arm. "I'd say my timing is most impeccable. Really, Luna, playing with a dog at a time like this."

Luna caught the jacket as it was tossed at her.

Wearing it would look kind of odd, though, with nothing else on.

"How did you find us?" Luna asked, letting her hand dart sideways to snatch at Jeoff's pile of clothes. While his briefs were a little large, they covered her bottom, and his T-shirt did a good job of hiding the rest. It didn't help with the chill, though. It wasn't exactly warm enough to be walking around in the buff, especially now that Jeoff had that closed-off look on his face.

So close to getting a taste. Ruined by Reba, who surely had cock-blocking down to a science.

"I was visiting my grandma. She lives just a few streets over. I came to check out the sirens and saw what's left of your bike."

"Left?" Forgetting she was still barefoot and wearing only a man's T-shirt and a coat, Luna went bolting, but she couldn't run fast enough to save her precious.

When Jeoff reached her, she was kneeling beside her bike, trying to stifle sobs. In the frenzy of the first responders, her precious baby had been knocked to its side and dragged out of the way to make room for the firemen and their hoses.

Ash layered it in a dirty film, hot embers had scored the hand-stitched leather seat, and the tank was scraped and dented from its ignoble abuse. She patted it. "It's okay, baby. Momma is going to make it all better."

"Is she all right?" a stranger asked.

Luna heard the whispered query, but didn't reply. Nothing would be all right until her baby was fixed.

Sob.

"She was very close to her bike," Jeoff replied.

"I saw you guys pull up on it. Were you the new tenants? Guess you won't be moving in now."

Luna half listened as she hugged her bike.

"Actually, we were friends of the couple who used to live here. We popped out to say hi, but noticed they were gone."

"Yeah, it was strange how quick they moved out. Petunia never said a word about them leaving."

"So you talked?"

Luna peeked from the corner of her eye and noted Jeoff, dressed in his pants, jacket, and wearing shoes, chatting to a petite redhead dressed in a tiny robe. A very tiny robe.

Grrr.

"I chatted with Petunia a few times. She was a hoot. She and her husband kept trying to get me and my boyfriend to go out with them."

"Go where?"

"Partying at the clubs. But we didn't go."

"Not into the club scene?" he prodded.

"Oh, I like partying, don't get me wrong, but Petunia wasn't into regular dance clubs. She and her husband were into kinkier stuff."

"How kinky?" Jeoff asked, his voice a low, husky whisper, and that little redheaded hussy—who obviously wasn't a very good girlfriend—sucked it up.

"Like really kinky, as in swinger clubs."

Goodness, now there was something Luna hadn't known.

"Really? I didn't know there were any of those around here."

"There's not many. Most are just a few couples getting together. But there was this one place. It's in the city, down in the warehouse district. She kept telling us we should go."

"Do you remember the name of this place? I know some friends who might be interested."

The redhead tapped her chin. "Ugh. I can't remember it. I do know it's a weird name. Kind of jungle and zoo-ish at the same time."

That was the only clue Luna needed. She jumped to her feet and joined the conversation. "Does Rainforest Menagerie ring a bell?" Luna had heard of it through the grapevine, but never gone. She preferred to do her partying within staggering and crawling distance of home. "Do you happen to know if they went there in the days before they disappeared?" Luna asked. But she might have done so a little too aggressively.

The redhead took a step back. "I don't know. It's not like I was keeping track of them. And what do you mean disappear? I thought they moved out."

Jeoff soothed the neighbor. "They did move. Doing great in their new place too."

"But I thought you said—"

"Can you excuse us? I think I see our friend waving to us from the street."

Indeed, Reba was waggling a hand at them, and Luna allowed Jeoff to steer her from her bike. She huddled in her coat, its warm interior doing nothing for her bare legs and feet.

"What's up, pussycat?" she asked.

"The cops want to talk to you and find out what happened." Reba inclined her head, and Luna couldn't mask a groan.

"Not the fuzz. They hate me."

"Gee, I wonder why," Jeoff remarked.

"Don't start with me, wolfie. I'm already in a bad mood."

"Your bike can be fixed. I know a guy. Leave it

to me and I'll have him take care of it."

"What about the cops, though? What are we supposed to tell them?"

Because they couldn't exactly hide the fact that they were both only partially dressed and at the scene of a crime. Her bike parked out front being the biggest clue.

"Let me handle this." He laced his fingers through hers, and they walked over to the pair of cops, one human, one not.

"Hey, Ralph. Clive." Jeoff gave both officers a nod.

"You know them?" she whispered.

"Of course I do. In my line of work, I sometimes have to collaborate."

"Jeoff, I meant to give you a shout and say thanks for that tip on the Peeping Tom. We nabbed the guy finally. Now the only thing he's showing his wang off to is the cameras downtown at the precinct."

"No problem. Always glad to help." Jeoff flashed a smile.

Clive, a bear Luna had run into before—usually because someone called the cops about the drunk girl—had a pad and pen out. "Care to tell us what happened here?"

"It was the most fucked-up thing," Jeoff said. "Luna and I were checking out this rental property, on account we're thinking of moving in together."

"You are?" Clive's brows rose. Hell, Luna's face probably showed some of the same shock at the smooth lie. "I didn't know you were dating anyone."

"Yeah, we've been keeping it quiet. But are now thinking of taking the next step, so we were checking out the place and testing the appliances, you know to make sure they worked. As you both know, I like to cook."

"Yeah, those rum balls you made for the Christmas party were amazing." Ralph rubbed his rotund belly.

"Anyhow, I guess the valve malfunctioned and the gas didn't shut off. We didn't know and took a peek at the backyard. When we went to step back inside, Luna hit the light switch by the back door and whoosh. The whole place lit up."

"So it was an accident?" Clive scribbled in his notebook.

"Totally. Really sorry about that. I wish I'd smelled the gas before we'd gone out."

"Well, that seems pretty cut and dried. I'll file the report. If you can come by and sign off on it at some point in the next day or two, that would be great." Clive flipped his notebook shut, but Ralph had a crease between his brows.

"Hold on a second, partner. I've got a few questions, like, where are the rest of your clothes? And why doesn't she have any shoes?" He pointed to Luna's bare toes.

She had an answer for that. "My boyfriend here is trying to protect my reputation. Such a sweetie." She giggled. "See, the real reason the stove accidentally stayed on is I might have accidentally grabbed and turned a knob when Jeoff was taking me like a wild beast on the counter."

Chapter Six

I can't believe she said that.

No, he totally could believe it. The real problem was, if he were a man with a little less control, it could have happened.

With the firemen in charge of the scene and the cops happy with their statement, they hitched a ride with Reba, who dropped them off on her way back to the condo. For some reason, Luna elected to stay with Jeoff, claiming they had business to discuss.

The only thing he wanted to talk to was a shower to get the stink of smoke off his skin. Since his place had two bathrooms, they could both shower at the same time, some faster than others. He was still rinsing off soap when she started talking to him.

"So, do you think Ralph bought our story?"

A peek around the shower curtain showed Luna wore a towel and nothing else where she sat perched on his counter.

"I'm sure Clive will make sure the facts fit. Did you really need to come in here and talk about it now?" He ducked back behind the curtain and turned the hot water completely off. No need for extra heat when she was around. Whenever Luna was near, his body tended to get feverish.

"Don't tell me you're still shy? I've seen it, wolfie. And I didn't laugh."

"No, you accused me of being a gibbering,

comatose playtoy."

"Only because you won't prove otherwise."

"Not happening." Not because he wasn't tempted. He was too damned tempted.

Press her against the wall and take her from behind. His wolf didn't care about repercussions. Primal need was very simple to his inner beast, and his need screamed he should claim her.

Like hell.

She was already causing chaos in his life—and this was just one day! He couldn't imagine a string of them, weeks, or months. Letting her into his world in anything other than a temporary work capacity would probably kill him—*but we'd die smiling, I'll bet.*

There was something about Luna that woke every nerve in his body. It made a man want to smoke some weed to dampen the high.

"So what's our next step, wolfie?"

"Your next step involves putting some clothes on. Grab a sweater or something from my closet."

"Again with the putting on of clothes. Are you always this obsessed about nudity?"

Only when she was around. Jeoff shut off the shower and reached blindly for a towel. Fabric met his fingertips, and he grabbed it, wrapping it around his waist, the towel warm and slightly damp—

"You gave me your used towel?" Not thinking, he secured the towel one-handed and yanked the curtain on the rail. Perched on his vanity, wearing only a smile, was Luna. Naked Luna. Being a man, a very put-upon man, he stared for a moment.

"Don't drool too much, wolfie. Wouldn't want you to slip and hurt yourself."

Why drool when he could lick? He'd lick that smile off her face by licking somewhere south until she had no breath to speak.

Well, she could say our name.

Moaning was all well and good, but sometimes a man liked to make sure she knew who to thank.

His tongue stayed in his mouth—sad whimper—and the towel remained around his waist, with no accidental flashing. As he strode past Luna, he did his best to look ahead, instead of at her ridiculously gorgeous breasts.

As if she'd let him get away with such nonchalance. Her foot shot out. He dodged to avoid it, loosening his grip on the towel, which she then tore from his grasp.

It wasn't, however, the sudden nudity that caused him to snap. It was the flick of the towel against his bare ass.

Technically, it didn't hurt much, just a light sting, but that little wee snap of wet towel still broke the wolf's back. He spun, grabbed Luna around the waist, and tossed her over his shoulder. He marched back to the bedroom and sat down. A bit of manhandling had her splayed across his lap, bottom raised, head down.

There were a few things a man could expect when putting a lioness in a punishment-type position. Contrition: *"Please, Jeoff, don't spank me. I'll be a good girl."*

From Luna? Not likely.

Anger: *"You son of a bitch, I'm going to feed you your balls."*

Much more Luna's style.

Even a savage wrestling match for dominance was something he totally expected from her. What he didn't expect was curiosity.

Luna peeked up at him. "What are you waiting for? Do it."

"Do what?" He questioned to be sure they were thinking the same thing. She was lioness; you never knew.

"Spank me. It is why you have me like this, isn't it?"

"You've been corrected before?"

"Corrected?" She snickered. "That's funny. And no. Never met a guy with the balls to try. So I've got to admit I'm kind of curious."

Which totally took all the fun out of it. Not to mention all this talk made him reevaluate his initial plan to pinken those cheeks with his hand.

He should note that he'd never spanked a woman before. Ever. Nor had he been spanked as a child. The only reason he thought of it was because of something one of the guys told him. Except, in his buddy's story, the girl didn't beg to be spanked and they'd ended up having wild sex.

No sex with this lioness. It wouldn't end well.

Want her.

Wolves shouldn't give puppy eyes. It just wasn't right.

All this pressure. He didn't like it. Setting Luna on the bed beside him, he rose and went to his dresser.

"Are you getting some kind of spanking aid? Can't we start with your hand? I don't know if I want to go right into a Ping-Pong paddle or a whip."

Turning around, he tossed a T-shirt at her. "Put this on. There is not going to be any kind of smacking."

"You are such a Debbie Downer."

"It's called being responsible. You should try it sometime."

Her head popped through the neck of the shirt, the tousled blonde hair hiding one eye. She squinted at him. "Responsibility is overrated."

"In that case, go home."

"Are you moping?"

"No. I am telling you to leave because you're lying. You are responsible. More than you think."

Luna shook a fist at him. "Take that back. I am a free-wheeling spirit. I do what I like when I like with no accountability to anyone."

"Except Arik."

"He's the king."

"And your family."

"Duh."

"Your friends."

"Your point?" she asked.

He leaned close and couldn't help but grin as he whispered, "You not only obey the king of your pride, you are helpful with your friends, and you're even determined to help strangers. You are a mature adult."

"Aaah." She made the sign of the cross at him and scowled. "Be gone, beast, with your foul words."

"Are you for real?"

"One hundred percent. No plastic in these. Give me a squeeze if you'd like to be sure."

"No." Bad enough she cupped her breasts in invitation. He stalked out of the bedroom, forgoing a shirt for the moment. He needed space between him and Luna. Alcohol too.

When he emerged from the kitchen, two beers in hand—because he knew she wouldn't leave that easily—she was perched on his couch.

"Toss it here." She held up her hands and waited.

He passed it to her carefully. One simply did not toss open bottles. She had her cell phone in her lap, the screen lit with a search window.

"What are you looking for?" He chose to sit on a barstool at his kitchen counter. Arguably, he could claim it was because his phone was sitting there getting juice from a charger. But, in truth, he needed the distance.

"I am looking for info on that club, but would you believe there isn't a damned thing on it?"

"Impossible. Maybe you're spelling it wrong."

Or maybe this place was hidden a little more than seemed normal.

The next few hours passed in oddly companionable silence, interspersed with anecdotes of what they'd found—or not found. At one point, he looked over to see her sleeping on the couch, lying flat on her stomach, one leg hanging down, mouth open on a soft snore.

Ridiculously cute. He wanted to stroke the hair from the curve of her cheek. Snuggle in behind her and hold her against his body, keeping her warm.

Instead, he tossed a blanket over her, turned off the lights, and went to bed. He didn't sleep, not right away at any rate, and when he did, there was a lot of chasing—a lion after a wolf, which culminated in a canine climbing a tree. Most disturbing, so was it any wonder at the sudden weight that bounced on his chest and the, "Wake up, wolfie," he let out a most beast-like, and ferocious, roar?

"Ooh, scary. Now wake up."

"No respect." He kept his eyes closed, lest he see her. "Why are you still here?"

"Because I spent the night."

"Don't you have a home you can go to?"

"Worried I might leave while we're still having fun? Never. I'm here for as long as you need me."

"Doesn't anyone need you at home?"

"Nope. All my plants are plastic, and the only pet I have is virtual, and probably starving. I haven't checked on it in a while."

"You should go home. You need clothes." Because he suddenly didn't want to loan her his shirt. Didn't want the fabric he wore close to his skin touching hers.

That's right, peel it off her. She's better off wearing nothing.

Jealous of his shirt. He must have had a few too many beers last night.

"So while you were sleeping the day away—"

"We went to bed after three."

"Lightweight. Anyhow, while you were playing Sleeping Beauty, I came to some interesting conclusions about our secretive club."

"Did we get some info finally?" he asked.

"No. They're still locked down tight. So, I'm going to check the place out in person."

"You're planning to infiltrate." The burst of jealousy took him by surprise. Why would he care if Luna dolled herself up and went undercover at a sex club for swingers?

"That is the plan, but here's the problem. If it's like most of the usual places for swingers, then it will be open for couples and single ladies only."

"And? I fail to see the issue. You're a single lady." Last he'd heard at least. Not that Jeoff kept dibs. He did his best to avoid the ladies of the pride—bad enough his sister felt a need to give him updates now that she lived among them.

"That's what I said to Arik. I told him I'd go check things out. But he seems to think I should bring backup, and, thing is, he said taking my besties with me wasn't a good plan."

Arik was a wise leader. Sending one lioness somewhere was asking for trouble. Once they grouped in a pair or more? No one was safe.

"So Arik doesn't want you to go by yourself. That still doesn't…" His voice trailed off as horror consumed him, a horror that grew deeper the more Luna smiled at him from her perch on his chest. He shook his head in vehement denial. "Oh no. Hell no. Not happening."

"But I haven't even told you why I need you. Other than for some obvious nookie to scratch an itch."

"You want us to go to that club and pose as a couple."

"Don't look at me with that horrified gaze. This was Arik's idea."

"When did you talk to Arik?"

"I've been up for a while."

And obviously high on caffeine or something if she'd agreed. "What else did he say?"

"He said we should go together as a committed couple. I then might have laughed at his idea. As if anyone would believe this is ready to settle down." She gestured to her shape, fingers skimming over her frame.

"The more unbelievable part is anyone thinking you and I could pass as a couple."

"We did it last night with the fuzz."

"For a few minutes. They were distracted, and we got away with it. But no way could we get anyone to believe we're truly together."

"What's that supposed to mean?" Luna asked, sounding most indignant.

"We couldn't be more mismatched. I mean,

I'm a suit kind of guy who likes reading and fine dining and a daily run in the park."

"First off, I'd totally run with you. After all, someone needs to hold the leash. I think books are great, especially for the times you run out of sand for the kitty litter box. And I love eating. Anytime you want to see my *eating* skills"—she winked—"you let me know."

"Has the chef at your condo been putting cat nip in the muffins again?"

"No." Her lips pulled down in a pout. "Apparently it's a gateway drug to squeaky mouse toys and drinking all the cream."

He closed his eyes as he pinched the bridge of his nose. "Why me?" Muttered aloud, so of course she heard.

"I think you're a great choice for a fake boyfriend because if anyone needs to get out and let loose, it's you."

"I have responsibilities."

"You do, and according to you, so do I." Her voice turned serious, a rarity for her, which made it all that more effective. "I need your help, but if you feel you can't, then I'll find someone else to play the part of boyfriend."

Someone else? Hell no. How could he subject some other poor bastard to the insanity that was Luna? "I'll do it."

"Really?" Her exuberant exclamation didn't prepare him for the way she grabbed him and hauled him to a sitting position.

Stronger than she looked. "What are you doing?"

She wrapped her arms around his neck. "Just getting my new fake boyfriend used to having me touch him. Can't have you flinching every time I do this." Leaning close, her warm breath fluttered across his skin.

He shivered and leaned away. Not because he wanted to. On the contrary, he wanted to feel her lips on his skin because that would provide the invitation for his hands to roam.

Roaming would lead to bad things.

Pleasurably bad things. So Jeoff dumped Luna from his lap before sliding from the bed and giving himself some space.

She grumbled. "This won't work if you keep acting so repressed."

"I am not repressed."

A challenging glint entered her eyes. "Prove it."

There were many things a man could fight against. He could guard himself against seduction. Hold himself in control instead of lashing out. Work out to burn calories after a night of too many beers. But prick at his manhood and something had to be done.

Before he could talk himself out of it, he snared Luna close with an arm curled around her waist. He drew her taut to him and lifted her on tiptoe so that her lips could come within a hair of his own.

"Don't worry about my acting skills in public," he whispered across her lips. "I'll play the part of loving boyfriend, so long as you can play the part of sane female. Of us two, I think your role will be harder to achieve."

With that, he released her, noting the O of surprise on her lips along with the annoyance—and heated interest—in her gaze.

Uh-oh. I think I might have made things worse. Screw the eye of a tiger. The gaze of a lioness was much more deadly.

Chapter Seven

Stalking into the pride's condominium complex—where most of the lions and a few stray breeds in the city chose to live—Luna found herself still flummoxed by Jeoff. The man knew how to get her inner kitten purring and how to bristle her fur, all in a single stroke.

Talk about out of the ordinary. Usually, Luna was the one putting men off balance. This reversal of roles didn't sit well at all. It also wouldn't last long. Once they found out what had happened to those missing folk, she could go back to lusting after Jeoff from afar.

Or I can use this opportunity to scratch that itch. And then move on to furrier pastures.

"Luna!" A chorus of voices shouted her name as she pushed through the second set of glass doors into the building proper. The condominium complex was the heart of the shifter community for this area. The headquarters, so to speak. But while the men thought they ran the business from their cute little offices upstairs, in truth, the real work was done down below in the lobby.

More than a few tawny heads lifted as amber gazes focused on Luna. She waved a hand in their direction. "Wassup, biatches?"

"About time you got here." Stacey waved at her. "Get your fat ass over here. We need you to settle something for us."

"Fat?" Luna grabbed both cheeks. "This is all steel, cow."

"For now," Nellie announced in an ominous tone. "We all saw what happened to your mother's ass after she had you."

The term voluptuous came to mind. It also brought back traumatizing memories of her daddy constantly grabbing her mother's bum—and the fact that he still did after almost thirty years of marriage. So perhaps taking after her mother wasn't a bad thing.

Sauntering in their direction, Luna noted her crew clustered in a circle and looked at something on the floor. "What do you have there?" she asked, pausing outside the ring and peering over them.

Two shoes sat in the circle. A red stiletto with thin straps and an evil arch. The other was a more sedate black pump covered in matte leather, sporting a thicker heel and a solid toe.

"Which ones should Melly wear on her date tonight?"

"Seriously? This is what's so urgent?" She rolled her eyes and pointed—at Melly's bare toes. "The answer is painfully obvious. She needs to wear those, but only after a pedicure so that her toes look pretty around his ears." Because dating was overrated. When Luna wanted a good time, she went out with her friends, and when she wanted a *good time,* she stayed in with whoever grabbed her fancy.

"She's right! I'm going to order in from that Chinese place down the street. We can have a buffet." Melly grinned and laughter flowed as ribald suggestions abounded.

Situation resolved, Luna vaulted over the back of the couch and wedged a spot for herself between the ladies.

Stacey leaned close and sniffed. "What's that smell?"

Another nose pointed in the air and sniffed. "Is that dog? Was someone feeding that stray again?"

"She's not a stray," Nellie replied. "She's Arabella, Hayder's mate."

"What a waste of a lion," sighed Stacey.

"Who cares? I wanna know who reeks of Eau de Puppy."

"My fault," Luna admitted. "I was hanging with Jeoff." Actually, she'd spent the night, but she'd save that wicked bomb for the right moment.

"Hanging with the wolf? Whatever for?" asked Stacey, her fine nose wrinkled. "Did he need a flea bath?" Despite the pride's close arrangement with the small local pack, there was a certain natural animosity between the feline and canine groups. Good-natured for the most part, but that didn't stop the jokes.

For a moment, Luna almost admitted the truth, that she and Jeoff were on the hunt for what was beginning to seem like a real conspiracy to abduct folks. Perhaps it was time to draw them in to help with the secret. But...

This was a secret. Not only had Arik told her to keep quiet, but Jeoff had too. And Jeoff, as head of the security firm, was the expert. There was a slight chance that someone in the pride was linked to the disappearances. If she told her crew and her crew blabbed, they might spook any possible suspect.

Keeping this a secret was the right and responsible thing to do, but she needed to tell the girls something.

"I smell like dog because I spent the night at the wolf's place." Technically true. "Jeoff and I will be spending time together for the next little bit"—also true—"as a couple." Imagine the whistling sound of a bomb dropping then *kaboom*!

For a moment, shocked silence prevailed, a short-lived silence. Squeals soon abounded.

"You're dating Mr. Prissy Pants?"

"A cat and a dog? What is this pride coming to?" someone else moaned.

"When you're done with him, can I have a turn?"

A snarl curled Luna's lip before she could stop it. The sudden spurt of jealousy was unexpected. There was nothing wrong with Nellie's question. Luna was well known for her short-term patience with men. Few lasted more than a few weeks. Her record with a guy was less than three months.

Only because I haven't met the right one yet. The one that wouldn't make her sneak out of his bed and erase her number from his phone.

"So when did this happen?" Stacey asked. "I didn't realize you two even talked."

"I'll bet they did all their talking with tongues." Nellie made kissing noises and mimed hugging an invisible man, which caused the rest of them to erupt into giggles.

"He's dating you?" Joan couldn't hide the shock in her tone.

"What's that supposed to mean?" Luna snapped.

"Just he's so, you know, proper and stuff." Joan shrugged. "And you're so…you know…you."

The remark was eerily close to Jeoff's. For some reason, Luna took offense. "Well, we are an item, and we're going out tonight."

"Where?" More than few of them asked.

"Some swanky club. He's picking me up in a few hours."

"What are you going to wear?"

"Clothes of course."

Stacey rolled her eyes. "Duh, clothes, but what kind?"

"What's wrong with what I have on now?"

Apparently there were plenty of things wrong with the items she'd stolen from Jeoff's closet. A good thing her crew was more than willing to help her— AKA torture and stuff her into a stupid dress that required shaved legs—so that when she came downstairs at nine p.m. that night, she was waxed in all the right places, plucked, hair teased, and face painted into whorish perfection. She looked like a high-priced call girl—in the red heels Melly had rejected. Heels that seemed determined to dump Luna on her ass.

The things she did for work. Arik better appreciate it. *Just like Jeoff better admire it.* Although she couldn't have said why that mattered.

Teetering into the lounge area, the buzz of conversation died as those crowded around her fake boyfriend turned for a peek.

Luckily no one in the lobby commented on the fact that she wore a dress. Even luckier, none of the lionesses were touching her date. *Paws off, he's mine.* At least for tonight he was, and she didn't mind admitting he looked good enough to eat. Jeoff looked like a geeky stud muffin in his slim-fitting slacks, royal blue button-up shirt, and dark jacket. The glasses, which totally rocked her the right way, sat high on his nose. He was missing a tie, but, all in all, he looked absolutely delicious.

As she strutted to him in the heels that clacked obscenely loud on the floor—no sneaking up on anyone while wearing those suckers—she showed no expression as he looked her up and down, but even he couldn't hide the shine of approval in his gaze.

"I didn't think you owned a dress."

"Watch it, dog, or you'll be leaving here without a tongue."

He smiled. "And wouldn't that be a waste, given what it's capable of doing?"

The innuendo caused her to stumble, or maybe it was the heels. Either way, she fell forward, but didn't need to rely on her feline ability to land on her feet because a certain wolf came to her rescue. He caught her and steadied her, the corners of his eyes crinkled in mirth. "Point. I think I just won that round."

"Are you keeping score?"

"Aren't you?" he asked.

Of course she was, and now that he'd gotten ahead by one, she'd have to get him back.

"Shall we?" He crooked his arm, and she linked her arm in it, and when the ladies who had hung around whistled and cat called, she extended a middle finger and blew them a raspberry.

"Later, biatches!"

"Was that necessary?" he asked as he held open the outer glass door for her. Did he think her incapable of opening it herself?

It's called manners. The arrogant men in her pride didn't always show them.

"Was what necessary?"

"Forget it. I'm surprised to see you went all out for this evening. How did it feel to have to put on clothes?"

"Not as bad as expected since the girls all agreed I should skip the bra, and the panties are the tiniest thong in existence."

"What?" He stumbled on the sidewalk. Poor wolfie, he just wasn't as graceful as a feline.

"I'm practically commando. Makes it easier in case we decide to hit a bathroom at the club for a little something-something."

"We are not going to have sex. We are going there to do a job." The words emerged clipped.

She laughed. "Relax. I'm not going to maul you." Until later. *Rowr.* "But I had to make the girls believe I was planning to. If we want this charade to work, then we need to be a couple in public, just in case there's a spy in our midst."

"Much as it pains me to say, that's possibly a good point. Although I find it hard to believe one of the pride could be involved in making our kind disappear."

"I'd rather not think it possible either." She'd hate to have to kill a friend. For some things, there was no forgiveness, no trial. Justice was applied swiftly to the guilty. "Let's hope no one we know is involved, but until we can be sure, I'd rather play safe for the moment."

"Being responsible again. You keep surprising me. I thought the lionesses were all about taking risks."

"Risks are fine when it's only us affected. When it comes to best serving those I consider under my protection, then I take safety very seriously. However"—she leaned closer—"when it comes to pleasure, don't worry. I am wilder than you can imagine," she purred.

He stumbled.

Awesome.

Something also beeped and lights flashed on a car parked at the curb.

"Don't tell me that's your car?" she muttered, totally caught in panty-wetting adoration. She loved her bike, don't get her wrong, but on chilly nights and rainy days, it would be nice to have the comfort of an enclosed vehicle. Like this one.

"It's mine."

His being a 2015 Ford Mustang painted a gorgeous cherry freaking red and highlighted with sparkling chrome. How unexpected. She would have presumed something a little more sedate from the uptight wolf.

Then again, what did she really know of Jeoff? Sure, he sported a hot bod that practically every woman wanted to jump—paws off, biatches—but at the same time, he was rather standoffish with the pride, especially the ladies.

Dates humans. Her inner feline practically sneered the remark. Or so he claimed because he didn't want drama.

A little drama is good for the heart. It keeps us strong.

Boredom, on the other hand, was truly dangerous. A bored beast was a reckless one. Luna found herself bored often.

Not around Jeoff, though. There were plenty of things interesting about him. For all his somewhat geek exterior—and really she was having a hard time as seeing those glasses as anything more than the sexiest accessory ever—there was nothing dorky about him.

If she ignored the suits and spectacles, just went on facts, what did she know about him? He ran a security firm employing an interesting mix of human and Lycan, members of his small pack over which he ruled as alpha. So he had balls, even if he worked for the pride. Some of the ladies claimed he played guitar in some band, another totally hot dude thing.

Remember the television. How could she ignore the fact that his DVR didn't have a single UFC fight taped? No hard-boiled cop shows. Not a single reality show where contestants lost their shit.

Yes, she'd snooped. How else was she supposed to find out more about Jeoff? Why she needed to know more was something to discuss with her shrink—over a beer. Her favorite bartender had to make it look as if he was working when he dispensed great life advice.

Drawing alongside the car, she couldn't help but run her fingers along the hood, caressing the smooth painted metal. She had total car envy.

Reaching for the door handle, Jeoff beat her to the chase, once again treating her like a lady—snicker. He opened the door for her and waited until she tucked her legs in before shutting it.

She couldn't help but admire the interior, maybe a little too much.

Opening the driver side, he paused and blinked down at her. "What are you doing in my seat?"

Luna grinned at him and held out a hand. "I'm driving."

"No, you're not. Move over."

"Ah, come on. Don't be a grumpy dog. I wanna see how fast this baby can go."

"I'd prefer to arrive alive."

"I'll have you know my driving skills are impeccable. I know my way around a stick shift." Her hand might have curled around the shifter knob, but her gaze was on a spot below his waist.

He cleared his throat. "The answer is still no. And as your make-believe boyfriend, I insist you listen, or I am going to call a halt to this farce right now."

"Over a car?"

He ran his hand down the outside of the car, stroking it in a way her skin envied. "Over this car, yes."

"I consider this cruelty to cats, just so you know," she grumbled as she slid back over into her seat.

"I'll make it up with a saucer of cream later."

"Really?" She perked in her seat.

"Ice cream. In public," he added.

"And you call us pussies," she muttered.

"Buckle in."

For a man who professed a love for his car and feared Luna hurting it, he drove like...well, like Luna did. Fast, furious, with sharp cuts across lanes, abrupt bursts of speeds, and sliding into slim, perfectly timed spots.

Luna found him fascinating to watch, his face intense, his hand in firm control of the shifter, the slight clench of the muscle in his thigh each time he had to work the clutch.

"So, what do you think we'll find in this club?" she asked.

"No idea. After you left, I managed to find another couple from the pack who visited it before."

"What did they say?"

"They say there's nothing odd about the place other than the fact it caters to those looking to add a little spice to their sex life. Apparently it's a hybrid joint catering to humans and shifters. So be careful about exposing your feline side."

"What, no showing of my claws? No getting down and furry on the dance floor?"

He shot her a look. *The look.* It didn't work, and she didn't need him telling her how to behave. "What else do we know?"

"Did you not study up on the place?" he asked.

She propped her feet on the dash, ignoring the fact that her short skirt slid up and that she probably flashed a trucker as they zipped past him. "Studying is for people like you. I'm just along as the muscle." Best to get that out of the way now.

"The muscle needs to get her dirty feet off my dash."

"You're worried about my feet?"

"Move them."

"If you insist." She shifted sideways and plopped them into his lap. "Better?"

His lips tightened, possibly in pain. The heels might have jabbed a little harder than necessary at his rebuke.

"So, what else have you found out?" she asked when he didn't say a word.

"I found out that you're even more annoying in close quarters."

That would have stung more if she'd not noted the bulge in his pants. And, yes, she'd looked.

Jeoff might want to dislike her, but a certain part of him felt differently, and that was the only part that really mattered in a guy. Except for his tongue...

"It's a wonder you ever get laid with that kind of attitude," she grumbled. "Unless..." She peered at him, not daring to think it, but she totally dared to say it. "Are you a virgin, wolfie? Is that why you're so shy?"

The car swerved, a little closer to the curb than it should have.

"Me? A virgin?" The words sputtered with incredulity. "Not even close."

"So you're a slut?"

"How about we stick to the lead we're following? Do you know anything at all about where we're going tonight?"

Of course she did, but having him summarize it might have revealed things she missed. Since he insisted, she recited the facts. "Rainforest Menagerie opened just over a month ago. According to searches, it's owned by one Gaston Charlemagne. No idea who he is. He didn't approach the pride, and no one has gotten close enough to him to check if he's human or not. We've done some background checks but come up empty-pawed. We show him emigrating here from France, but beyond that, he's an enigma. Our overseas connections have nothing for us."

"And he set up his business right in the heart of the city. On that basis alone, I would think, if he was one of us, then we'd know by now."

Would they? Luna couldn't help but think of the clever person eating asparagus to mask their scent and the guy they chased through the woods. A guy who moved faster on two feet than a human should, but who didn't smell like a shifter. *However, that doesn't mean he wasn't some kind of shapeshifter.* Someone determined to hide who they were could do so, especially with the ease of getting scents online.

"What else did you find out about this place? The folks I spoke to confirmed it caters mostly to couples, but allows a certain ratio of single gals in. As to the clientele itself, there was human and shifter alike. Feline and Lycan mostly, but Barry said he spotted a bear with a human date when he went with his wife. Apparently, they flew in to party at the club."

"People are traveling in just to check out this place?" Exactly what kind of *extras* did this club offer?

"In the short time the place has been open, it's

achieved quite the reputation."

"And they let just any couple in?"

"I guess we're going to find out because we're here."

The street outside the club was crowded, very crowded. Cars lined both sides of the street, meaning Jeoff had to park several blocks away, illegally she might add.

"Someone is going to tow your ass," she said, pointing at the hydrant.

"No they won't." He flashed her a smile as he leaned toward her, close enough that his masculine scent swirled around in a heady mix. She could see herself reflected in his eyes as he reached between the seats to grab something.

Talk about giving a girl false hope.

He slapped an On Duty sign in the window.

"I need one of those."

"Don't you dare think of stealing mine," he growled.

She grinned. "Would I do such a thing?"

"Yes." How well he already knew her. Before he stepped out of the car, he said, "I assume you can handle a little walk."

In these heels? "I'll make it."

She never even made it to the sidewalk. Standing on the grate, more like stuck in it, her heel held prisoner by the metal, she wondered why she'd let those damned felines dress her like a girl.

Probably because I am a girl.

Hear her rowr!

However, she should have drawn the line at the shoes. Usually, the places she visited didn't mind if she wore torn jeans, a T-shirt insulting a group of people, most often blondes like herself, and running shoes—

or shit kickers if she thought she might have to give someone the boot.

But for tonight's excursion, she'd wanted to look pretty…for Jeoff.

Cough. Gag. Gasp. The realization had her wheezing, enough that when Jeoff made it around the car, he put an arm around her. "Are you all right?"

"Yes." Fine. Just fine except for the fact that she liked a stupid dog and wanted to impress him. The shame of it. "Just got my foot caught."

"You just couldn't wait for me to give you a hand." Jeoff peered down at her dilemma and then back at her with a shake of his head.

"I am perfectly capable of opening a car door and getting out myself."

"Apparently not." His mocking gaze went to her foot. She yanked it free, took a step, and found both her heels wedged in the stupid grate.

Her low growl of annoyance made him chuckle. "This is your fault."

"How do you figure that? I'm not the one wearing the most asinine footwear."

"You parked here on purpose."

"Yes, I did, so you would get stuck because that's the kind of guy I am."

The mocking didn't help, but rather intensified the heat of her glare.

"Let me give you a hand." He proffered it, but she, being a rather proud lioness, eschewed it. She would get free herself, thank you very much.

The first heel came free with relative ease. The second, not so much.

A yank of it caused a rather discernible cracking sound. The shoe came free, the heel did too, and it fell with a mocking splash somewhere below the grate.

Acting as nonchalant as possible—a cat trait that came in quite handy—she stepped onto the sidewalk with only a small, lopsided wobble. Would anyone notice?

Click. Clunk.

"Give me your foot," he ordered.

"No."

"Give it."

"Still no. I'm fine." *Click. Thunk.* She took a pair of lurching steps.

"Stubborn. So fucking stubborn." Said on a sigh.

In between one breath and the next, she found herself tossed over his shoulder, head down, ass up, fists clenched and pummeling.

"Put me down."

"In a second. Hold still while I get these off and your other shoes on you."

She stilled. "What other shoes?"

"The ones in my pockets. Someone slipped them in when I wasn't looking back at the condo."

"Let me see."

"You'll see them once they're on your feet."

Since he seemed determined, she let him swap her footwear. Anything was better than those damned heels. She should have told Melly to wear them.

The strappy sandals were removed and replaced with—she peeked at her feet in astonishment as he set her upright again. "Flip flops?" Fancy ones with rhinestones.

"Apparently your friends predicted we might have issues."

That would be Reba. At least she'd chosen sandals that could pass as sexy eveningwear. They weren't, however, meant for the mud on the sidewalk from an empty lot under construction. Before she could detour in the street, she found herself airborne again and carried princess style. The novelty proved entertaining. Usually, when she was getting forcibly removed, it was thrown over a shoulder by Leo or one of the other guys in the pride with her kicking and screaming invectives.

But Jeoff was treating her as if she were dainty.

Dainty! Thankfully, none of her crew lurked in the vicinity to point and laugh.

Since he seemed determined, she took advantage and nestled her nose against his neck for a sniff.

"What are you doing?" There was that hint of exasperation she loved to achieve.

"Smelling you."

"For what?"

"Just in case you get lost."

"Why would I get lost?"

"You're a dog. It happens all the time. Or don't you pay attention to the posters on the poles outside?"

"There are just as many feline ones, I'll have you know."

She nipped him. Hard.

We should scratch him too. Leave a mark.

"Ow, what was that for?"

"Do I need a reason?"

"Lions," he grumbled instead of replying. Once they reached a clear section on the sidewalk, he didn't immediately set her down.

She squirmed in his grip. "I can walk, you know."

"I do know, but if I'm carrying you, then you

are less likely to get in trouble."

"I'll have you know I do not get in trouble that often."

"I heard about the brawl at the Lion's Pride Steakhouse."

"That bitch totally deserved the drink I poured on her head. She made the waitress, who happens to be my cousin three times removed, cry." Nobody messed with Luna's family.

"And the night you spent in police lockup for disturbing the peace?"

"You heard about that?" She smiled. "Not my fault we live in a repressed society. All Joan and I were trying to see was if that expression 'nipples that could cut glass' was real. It was chilly that day. And we were both sporting some awesome beamers. Stupid prudes called the cops. Indecent exposure my ass."

As they got closer to the club, the distant thump of music vibrating in the air, he finally set her down. Linking her arm in Jeoff's, they managed to look very couple-y as they strolled toward the club, just another dirty couple looking for action.

Located down in the warehouse district, two and three-story buildings, big and squat and dark, loomed. Most of them appeared closed this time of night, and if it weren't for the club, it would probably be deserted. The predator in her noted the shadows and possibly spots for ambush. Awareness was the most important route to survival.

Since Jeoff didn't seem inclined to talk, she did. "Place looked busy. I saw a line as we drove by." She'd also noticed much sluttier outfits than hers.

"Afraid we won't be one of the cool kids let in to the place?"

"Oh, they'll let me in."

Except the guy didn't seem too inclined initially. He looked down at Luna, literally down from his like seven-foot height. Built like a mega beast, yet he didn't smell like a shifter. His cologne—which closely resembled pine-fresh air freshener for the car—practically burned the nose, and this guy, one step above simians, thought he should prevent her entry.

"No I.D. No entry." The big dude crossed his arms and sneered down at her.

Since when was I.D. a requirement to get into a club? Luna never brought any with her. Shifters tended not to in case they went for a run. Only an idiot left their personal effects lying around for someone to steal.

Jeoff came to her rescue. "I assure you, she's over the age of majority."

"Usually, I might take offense at someone calling me old, but this one time, I'm gonna allow it," she muttered. He could thank her for the magnanimity later.

"Maybe she is. But maybe she isn't," rumbled the bouncer. "I've seen sixteen-year-olds who look older than her. Sorry. No go."

Since Jeoff seemed determined to argue with the guy some more—because that was soooooo working—Luna bypassed him and resorted to her usual *modus operandi*.

Snaring the big bouncer's shirt in two fists, she gave it a tough yank, drew him down to her level, and kept him there.

"Listen up, big boy." She whispered the words, spoken softly, gently, but she knew the expression in her eyes was anything but. "You are going to stop pissing me off right now and let me in this club. You want to let me in this club. Because, if you don't, I got a crew of kitties capable of treating you to a hissy fit that will leave permanent marks on your back and ruin you for all other women."

"How are you so strong?" he asked.

She tugged him closer. "You don't want to know."

"She's right, you don't," Jeoff added. "Trust me on that."

"Now, are you going to stop pissing me off and let me in?" she asked.

Eyes wide, the bouncer nodded. It could have had to do with the pinprick of her claws. Or the wad of cash Jeoff slipped the guy.

"Thanks, bud." Jeoff kept his hand firmly in the middle of her back and pushed her toward the doors.

"I had that under control."

"You can't threaten everyone we need to talk to."

"I wasn't threatening. Just making a promise."

"From now on, let me handle the talking."

"I can see what kind of relationship this is going to be," she grumbled.

"A short-lived one if you don't behave. I don't suppose there is any point in telling you to behave."

"Depends, will you spank me if I don't?"

"Would it matter?"

She blinked at him. "Of course it would. If you promise to paddle my ass if I'm bad, then I will do my damnedest to misbehave. But I'm beginning to think you're all talk, no action."

With that, she blew him a kiss, winked, and then sashayed through the club doors.

What she didn't expect was the hard slap on

her butt as he caught up to her!

Chapter Eight

Unlike most girls, Luna didn't squeal when he gave her the smack on the butt she deserved. Instead, she uttered a husky laugh and grabbed at his arm.

"Not bad. I didn't mind that at all. But I'm pretty sure you can do better."

"You're a brat." A misbehaving lioness that he was taking into a couples-only club filled with a deep, booming bass that called to his wild side. *Must resist.* Nothing good ever happened when the beat took over and made a man resort to his more primal side.

The bouncer was apparently only the first layer of security. The next one involved beautiful young women with clipboards, who took aside anyone entering who didn't wear a wristband.

"Welcome to club Rainforest Menagerie," the petite redhead announced. "My name is Candy, and since you're new to the place, I just need you to fill out this teensy tiny form, make sure you understand the rules, and then you can go inside."

"What kind of rules?"

Trust Luna to ask, probably because lionesses preferred to make up their own.

"Just basics. Respecting other clients in the club. Promising to not drug other members or do anything that might coerce them into acting in ways they usually wouldn't."

Boiled down, the rules amounted to don't be a

dick and no meant no. The 'List your interests and activities' form, on the other hand, proved a lot more interesting.

Jeoff had to wonder at the questionnaire they had to fill in. Seated beside him on a pleather-covered bench, Luna leaned over to whisper, "It wants to know how often we do it." One of the tamer questions. She cast a sly look at the guard keeping an eye on them. "Should I count the BJs I give you in the shower or just the sex?" She batted her lashes at Jeoff, and he thanked the fuck he held the clipboard over his dick. Damned woman knew how to get him going. And by going, he meant harder than the fucking steel beams keeping most buildings upright.

The sex question was just the tip of the iceberg. It wanted to know sexual orientation. If they were into swapping. Or voyeurism.

It was the strangest thing Jeoff had ever filled out. But once it was done, and he'd paid their club fee—which he was going to bill Arik for—he and Luna were given their own bracelets and allowed entrance into the next level of the club.

The vestibule was moderately crowded, the dim lighting allowing them to see the coat check girl. Jeoff opted to keep his jacket. Luna whipped off the shawl, and he truly got a glimpse of her outfit.

I think she's missing part of it.

Surely something went over the corset, the sleek black lace cinched tight around her ribs, plumping her breasts over the top, barely contained by the thin silk chemise she wore under it. The tops of her shoulders were bare, as was the strip of flesh between corset and her hip-hugging skirt. A skirt under which she wore, by her own admission, only a scrap of fabric.

A true dog would have stuck his head under that teasing swath of a fabric for a peek. As a wolf of a certain number of years, he would do the right thing and wait until she bent over.

Luna and the coat check girl exchanged the shawl for a ticket, a ticket that got shoved into a shadowy valley.

"I have pockets, you know." A front one that she could have groped later in search of the ticket stub. He shoved his hands into the pockets.

"But this way you'll have to help me find it." Wink. She linked her arm in his before guiding them toward the double doors, manned by another bouncer, that led into the club proper. "Let's go have some fun."

"We're here to look for clues."

"Doesn't mean we can't enjoy ourselves while doing it."

The portal swung open, and a tsunami of sound washed over them, loud and thick enough to practically grasp and shape. Teeth vibrated at the deep bass. Skin hummed as well. It was noise, pure and simple, and yet there was something about the vibrating pulse, a primal instinct within its percussion that called to him. Called to Luna and everyone else in the place.

Movements turned into dance, not because they meant to, but more because you couldn't help yourself. Each step had a shimmy. Each strut forward a bit of a wiggle. The song demanded worship, and the body had to answer.

It wasn't the insistent call of the music that froze him into place, but what he saw beyond the doors. For a moment, he was tempted to turn around. *I don't belong here.*

Screw the conversation he'd had earlier with Arik.

"I am not taking that psychotic feline with me."

"Yeah you are, but to soften the blow, I'll double your usual rate. I'd rather she go with you than by herself."

Because Luna on her own was not something to contemplate. A place like this was a little more than he wanted to contemplate. Perhaps he was that prude Luna accused him of being.

This is a job. Get over it.

Luna didn't seem bothered by their surroundings. She linked her fingers in his and tugged him in her wake. They made it a fair distance past the door, the inside busy but not wall-to-wall packed. Movement was still possible and some space still available between the gyrating bodies. While other bodies were so close it seemed like one.

They remained on the edge of the dance floor. Leaning against a pillar, Jeoff didn't stiffen—much, at any rate—when Luna turned into him and stood on tiptoe. She grabbed his head, bringing her lips to his ear. The impression was one of intimacy. "Looks normal so far. Kind of disappointing, if you ask me."

He nuzzled her neck, letting the smoking of his lenses hide the fact he avidly watched the room. He let his lips roam to her ear, playing the part of besotted lover. It wasn't hard to pretend. "Depends on your idea of normal. Most clubs don't have people making out in cages." He should note that he couldn't actually see them. The thin gauzy material over the cage projected only their shadows, but what that shadow did... Definitely X-rated.

Laughter bubbled as she replied. "Then you don't know where to hang out."

No, what he knew was he preferred to keep his

private matters private. He didn't understand why people would want to act out intimate fantasies in public. Too many eyes on him made his fur itch, just like too many eyes on Luna's shapely figure made him bristle.

Mark her and they'll know she's ours.

His wolf was really getting tiresome with its suggestions.

"I don't think we're going to find anything standing here." Other than a possible need to suddenly visit a clinic for some shots, as some human, wearing naughty leather shorts and a leashed collar, bumped into him.

Hands pressed against his chest, Luna presented a smile at him, a sweet smile tainted by a mischievous glint in her eyes. "I see Mr. Prude is back. You've got that look in your eyes."

"What look?"

"The look that says the folks having fun in that cage should get a room."

"I don't see what's wrong with having a little modesty."

"Modesty is for those who have something to hide." She shuffled closer, the length of her body pressing against his.

It was taunts like these that made him think modesty be damned and act out of character. Dares like the one in her eyes that made him grab her hand and press it against the front of his pants. "You should know by now that I have nothing to be ashamed of." And he should know better than to try to think he could shock Luna.

Where another girl might've squealed or slapped him, or even giggled, Luna just had to set herself apart. She squeezed his package, tilted her chin, and got a thoughtful look on her face as she mused aloud. "Seeing and touching, two different things. So let's see what we have here." Squeeze. "Decent girth." Rub. "Excellent reaction to stimulus. Lengthy too, which is always a bonus. Overall, not too shabby."

Not too shabby. There was a compliment to make a man want to hide himself. Before she could embarrass him further, or insult his manhood to the point that it shriveled past repair, he grabbed her hand. "Let's go grab a drink."

This time, he led the way, weaving through the bodies, dodging the pillars with shelves wrapping around and couches where men sat with women straddling their laps. He was pretty sure more than one skirt was hiding some naughty action.

To his surprise, he noticed a guy from his pack on one of the couches—along with a woman who wasn't his wife. It bothered him. He never understood people who strayed from their mates. In his world, once you made a commitment to someone, that commitment meant something. His word meant something.

How could you betray *the one* once you found her?

We will be true to the female.

What female? And yet, did he really need his wolf to answer? It still suffered under some crazy misconception that Luna meant something. A lioness, belong to him? Only if he had her stuffed and mounted. Those wild ladies were hard to pin down, and even if you did get one to call your own, forget having a life. He'd need another job for bail money.

They hit the bar. He grabbed a beer from the frazzled bartender while Luna got something with an umbrella. Turning around, he leaned against the bar to

71

peruse the room. Luna leaned against him, her closeness a distraction he couldn't shake.

"See anything?" he asked in a low tone, knowing she'd hear him. Excellent hearing was something most shifters had.

"Lots of folks making out. But nothing that screams psycho killer is casing the joint to kidnap people."

He sighed. "We are making a few assumptions here. For one thing, we don't know there's a killer."

"But folks are disappearing, and under odd circumstances. You seem to be claiming we shouldn't jump to conclusions. Then what should we jump to? Why are we here if you don't think there's a link?"

Why indeed? It wasn't as if they could flash pictures of the missing folk and question everyone here. It would blow their cover, and he didn't want to do that quite yet. "That tiger couple were known to come here, and so was my missing wolf couple. We can't be sure about the third pair. I'd say two out of three is a pretty strong coincidence, but at the same time, we can't go off half-cocked. What if we're wrong?"

"What if we're not? What if the owner of this place is involved in some kind of scheme involving swinging shifters?"

A possibility. He'd heard of shifter trafficking happening in other states, but it wasn't common. The fact that the disappearances had started around the same time this club opened was interesting, though.

"We're not going to figure anything out just standing here," she observed. True. He let her grab him by the hand and lead him from this large chamber through a wide arch into a second one, where the music was still just as loud and the space even more packed with bodies.

In here, there were no chairs or couches to lounge on. The ceiling overhead sparkled with dancing colored lights projected by disco balls. Along the left wall of the room stretched a long bar with no stools. People leaned against it, some nursing drinks, some just standing and staring at those gyrating on the dance floor.

Here the separation of couples was less distinct, as bodies undulated in a mass frenzy, moving freely with the music.

"I'm going to go deep. You keep watch." Before Jeoff could say no, Luna shimmied away from him, thrusting herself in the midst of the moving and grooving bodies. Since he had no intention of joining her, Jeoff tossed back the rest of his beer and headed to the bar. In his experience, that was usually the best place to find information.

He found himself a spot at one end of the counter for the bar. It took only a moment for the bartender tending this section—a big, dark-skinned fellow wearing only jeans that hung low on his hips, leaving his impressively muscled torso bare—to note him.

The bartender placed his hand on the bar and leaned forward with a smile, his teeth a gleaming white with the exception of one capped in silver with a symbol etched on it. This close, Jeoff could smell bear; the bartender was definitely a shifter, a grizzly, he'd wager.

"What can I do you for?" asked the bartender.

"I'll take whatever you have on tap." Jeoff leaned an elbow on the bar, the picture of nonchalance as he let his gaze dance over the crowd, easily spotting Luna's blonde mop bopping amidst them. She didn't dance alone. On the contrary, she found herself surrounded by two women and two men. A lioness playing in the middle. It didn't seem to bother her that there was a lot of bumping and grinding going on, as well as inappropriate sliding of body parts.

It didn't bother her, but it sure as hell bothered him. Why? Luna was a grown woman. If she wanted to dance, she could dance. If she wanted to let those perverts touch her, that was her prerogative too.

No touching. Bite them.

His wolf sounded just as annoyed as him. It didn't help that his mind kept trying to make him realize something. Nope. He wouldn't let it. For the moment, denial was his best friend.

The bartender placed a glass in front of him filled almost to the brim with a golden liquid topped with a hint of froth. Jeoff noted nobody else trying to vie for his attention, so he thought, what better time to try to strike up a conversation? "I'm Jeoff."

"Malcolm," offered the man behind the bar.

"Hey, Malcolm. This is my first time here, and holy shit, I gotta say, this place is fucking busy."

"No shit. Of late, it's been like this almost every single night. We've got people coming to see us from all over the country. Apparently, we are the number one spot for swingers. I take it you're here with your old lady?"

Wouldn't Luna freak if she heard Malcolm call her old. "Yeah. She's a frisky thing. Always dragging me out to try new shit." Frisky being an understatement.

"Nothing wrong with a little spice."

This went beyond a little spice in his mind. "You been working here long?" he asked.

The bartender shook his head. "Nope. Just

started last week. I was actually headhunted from a place I was working out on the West Coast. They made me an offer to come and bartend. Crazy shit, eh? Whoever heard of a bartender getting headhunted? But the money is good. And the tips even better." Was that a subtle hint? Jeoff tossed a twenty down. The bartender smiled and tucked it in the waistband of his pants.

"So other than this room and the one with the couches, what else can I expect?"

"You should explore and find out. I wouldn't want to ruin the surprise for you. This club is a wonderland for the erotic senses."

"I thought I saw a second floor. What's up there?"

Malcolm shook his head. "Second floor is off-limits to guests. Management office and shit. Boring stuff. Don't worry, there's plenty of stuff to keep you entertained right here."

Plenty, indeed, given Luna sashayed her way back to him, lips shining and parted, body undulating in ways that made people watch.

He could lie all he wanted and say the reason he reached out for her was to show his fake claim, to keep up the pretense of their so-called relationship. In truth, he drew her close because he wanted to. Plain and fucking simple. He liked having her near him, touching him.

"I see someone's finally loosening up. Come on. Let's dance."

Jeoff really didn't want to, but Luna left him no choice. She tugged him by the hand, dragging him onto the dance floor. Resistance was futile, especially once she placed her hands on his hips and began to gyrate against him.

The lights continued to flash, and they refracted and twinkled as they lit sparkles of dust drifting down upon them. The glitter coated his skin, got in his mouth, inhaled with every breath. No scent. No taste. Just another gimmick employed by a club to entertain the patrons.

Despite Jeoff's reluctance, his hips moved, his hands spanned Luna's waist and kept her near. The scent of her surrounded him.

She smells so damned good.

The closeness of her body, the heat burning between them, made it hard to remember why he was here. He had a purpose.

Yes. Take the female. That is our purpose.

No, there was another reason he was here. Something other than the way her parted lips invited and the grind of her pelvis against his made him want to spin her around and take her. Here and now.

Madness. They were in public, a fact he clung to. He tried distraction by looking elsewhere, checking out the crowd, but everywhere he looked, people were clinging to each other, kissing and groping.

As a matter of fact, he and Luna were the only ones not engaged in a torrid embrace. It excited. It bothered. He grabbed her by the hand and returned to the first room, the room with the couches and, hopefully, a semblance of sanity.

He didn't find any. In fact, in here things had gotten very naked and sweaty. Surely the acts going on were not allowed by law? The whole place seemed to have gone wild, succumbed to carnal need.

And still the lights flashed and the dust sparkled.

Around him, eroticism abounded, and although he fought to retain his senses and morals, in the end, Jeoff discovered he wasn't immune. When Luna grabbed him by the cheeks and kissed him, he didn't stop her. On the contrary, his blood heated to the boiling point when her tongue made a sensual foray into his mouth.

Surrendering to the moment, he let his hands stray. He cupped her full ass, pulling her tight against him, pressing her against his body. A wildness burned in him. A need to have this woman.

Take her now.

Yes. Yes. She was his. *Mine.* He just needed to sink into her.

As his hands delved under her short skirt, he let his mouth burn a trail down her neck, sucking at the tender skin. At a loud moan, not his or Luna's, his eyes shot open, and he caught a glimpse of other couples around him, none of them even making a pretense of dancing as they hit the floor in a frenzy of limbs and thrusting hips.

A part of him recognized this wasn't normal. He didn't feel in control of himself, and that realization was enough to bring some sanity back.

This isn't right. This isn't normal.

He grabbed Luna's hand and made for the exit, not the one they'd come in, but the closest one he saw, the red letters promising escape. As he shoved open the door, a beeping alarm went off, but the crisp rush of cool air flowing in did a lot to help clear his head. But it did nothing to help those still inside.

"Hey, you're not supposed to use that door." A fellow dressed in unrelieved black, with a lanyard and badge declaring he was staff, grabbed the door and blocked their exit. He glared at Jeoff, the tip of his cigarette dangling from his mouth, gray smoke curling from it.

"Just the thing I need," Jeoff remarked. He snagged the burning cigarette and slipped back inside, ignoring the "What the fuck are you doing?" from the guy.

What he was doing was putting an end to the five-alarm orgy by declaring a one-alarm fire. The city insisted on businesses adhering to their fire codes, and one of them insisted on smoke alarms, lots of them, especially in places like these where folks liked to sneak a few puffs of Mary Jane or something a little stronger.

Snaring a stray napkin from the floor, Jeoff ignited it with the lit tip of the cigarette. It immediately began to smoke, the acrid stench reviving him from the erotic pull that still existed in the club. He dropped the burning napkin into a waste bin and returned to the door to find Luna leaning against it, standing over the inert body of the bouncer.

"Please tell me you didn't kill him." The paperwork would suck.

"Nope, just got him to sleep on the job." She grinned at him. "Idiot never saw it coming."

Humans never expected to get taken down by someone they thought weaker than them. They saw a petite blonde, with a devilish grin and a tight body, and never expected her wicked left hook. Apparently, Luna was champion when it came to knocking folks out. Or so rumor claimed. Jeoff preferred to not experience it for himself.

As he exited through the door, an alarm sounded, strident in pitch. More unexpected, though, was the sprinklers that turned on, dousing the room in a cold shower. As sanity returned under the chilly deluge, he heard at least one person exclaim, "What the fuck just happened?"

What the fuck indeed.

Exiting into the alley, he let the door slam shut behind him, but he doubted it would remain closed for long given what he'd done.

Eyes somewhat glazed and her lips swollen from the kiss, Luna frowned as she swayed on her feet. "What's wrong with me?" The words were slightly slurred. "Did you feed me a roofie?"

"Not me, but I think someone in the club did." He curled an arm around her waist. "Come on. Let's get out of here."

Luna leaned into him as they moved up the alley between buildings. Behind them, he heard the door slam open, hitting the building's brick wall. A cacophony of noise filled the night air as people spilled out with excited chatter.

Turning the corner, he and Luna left them behind and, for the second time in as many days, heard the distant sound of sirens.

Luna stumbled, and his arm tightened around her. "You okay?" he asked.

"No. Someone drugged me." She sounded most put out.

"Someone drugged all of us."

"But how? I mean, I only had a few sips of my drink. Other people in there were drinking way longer, and yet we all started acting crazy at the same time."

"I don't know what it was." But he suspected a certain glittery dust. "Maybe there was something in the air." A something he didn't scent because of all the perfumes and sweat already masking odors in the place.

She turned in his arms, placing her hands on his chest. "Do you think what happened is related to the missing couples?"

"I don't know. I mean, getting a room full of people to decide to have an orgy is a far cry from kidnapping and wiping all traces of them."

Her nose wrinkled. "I was like a pussy in heat. If it weren't for you, we might have gotten down and dirty. How come you weren't affected?"

He'd blame the lingering drugs for saying, "I was affected, but I will note that I don't need any drugs to get horny around you."

The words escaped, and he wanted to take them back, except…a brilliant smile illuminated her face. "Why, wolfie. That is like the nicest thing you've ever said. You do like me."

"Do not." He lied. Then sighed. "Okay, I do like you, but this doesn't mean I've changed my mind about getting involved with you. I still think it's a bad idea."

She chose to ignore his negativity. She giggled as she grabbed his cheeks. "Bad ideas are usually the most fun, though." She kissed him, and he couldn't help but respond. Couldn't help but let his mouth slant over hers, tasting her, wanting her, needing her—and wondering if it truly was him she wanted or the drugs still talking.

Argh. He tore his mouth from hers. "We shouldn't be doing this. Not here. Not now."

"You're right. We should go back to your car. It'll be more private since you're such a prude."

"We are not having sex in my car."

"Yeah, I guess that might be a hard smell to get out of the leather. Your place it is, unless you've changed your mind and don't mind using this wall?" She splayed herself against it, an inviting smile curving her lips.

He almost said fuck it and fucked her. She

tempted him that damned much. He tore his gaze from her and took a few steps in the direction of his car. The snicker of her mirth didn't slow his steps, but the abrupt cessation of it saw him whirl.

...in time to catch the body hurtling at him.

Chapter Nine

As soon as the hand darted from the shadows, the body hidden between buildings, she didn't think; she acted. She grabbed the wrist and yanked, propelling the fellow forward with more force than necessary.

Jeoff caught the guy easily and dangled him. Then shook him. "What the hell do you think you're doing?"

"I need her." The dude with the glazed eyes practically moaned the words.

"You can't have her. She's with me."

Sexy words. Now if only Jeoff meant them.

"Were you in the club?" she asked, taking a step closer. The guy's nostrils flared, and his lips parted as his hands reached for her.

They never connected. Jeoff slapped him against the wall, hard enough to rattle the metal siding. "She asked you a question, perv. Were you in the club?"

"Yeah. Great place. I had sex," he confided in a whisper. "With another dude's wife."

"What of your girlfriend or wife?" Luna asked with a frown.

"She was there, too, getting her pussy—"

Jeoff shook him before the guy could finish that thought. "You're of no use to us. Go find your partner and go home. In a cab," he added as he sent the fellow stumbling on his way.

They both spent a moment watching the guy weave.

Jeoff shook his head. "I see the fresh air didn't clear his mind. Whatever was in the air must hit humans harder."

"I would have snapped him out of it with my fist, you know. You didn't have to shake him like a rag doll."

"Save your knuckles. We're going to need them."

"We are?" Sure enough, as they approached his car, she noted the trio of guys hovering by the Mustang. "Oooh, can I handle this?" she asked. "I've got some frustration to work out." Serious sexual frustration, but hitting something would ease some of that.

"Is this seriously how you want to end this evening? You, punching out guys?" He sighed. "Stupid question. Of course it is."

Speaking of the car, they'd reached it, and pulling out his keys, Jeoff hit the unlock button, which made the lights flash. He might as well have waved a red cape because the leader of the waiting trio stepped forth to utter a menacing, "Hand over those keys and your wallets."

"Is it just the three of you?" she asked, letting her senses roam to see if anyone else hid in the shadows. "That seems kind of unfair."

"If your boyfriend here hands over his keys and wallet, then no one has to get hurt."

"Oh, I wasn't talking about it being unfair to us." She smiled. "More like I was hoping for a little more sport."

"Think your puny boyfriend can take us?" The thug laughed.

"Me?" Jeoff shook his head. "Nope. I already told the lady she could have you. Just watch the car."

"If you think using your girlfriend as a shield is going to protect you—"

"Hold on to that thought for just a second." Luna held her hand up in the thug's direction. Peering back at Jeoff, she frowned. "Are you more worried about your car than little ol' me tangling with these boys?"

He arched a brow. "Are you trying to force me to insult you by claiming you can't handle them?"

"Listen, you fuckers, I said hand over the keys."

Both Luna and Jeoff shot a glare at the would-be carjacker. Luna growled. "I said to hold on. I'm not done talking to my friend here."

"Talk later, bitch."

"Oh you did not just say that," she breathed, her eyes lighting with excitement.

"Oh you did not just say that," Jeoff groaned.

"I'll be back in a second." Luna kicked off her flip-flips and then beckoned to the lead thug with her fingers. "Here, idiot, idiot." She sang the taunt.

"I'll teach you to—Argh. Eeee. Ohhhh."

Luna never did find out what he wanted to teach her unless it was how to achieve a certain pitch when the pain reached a crescendo. It might have had to do with the fact that she hauled his head down and brought her knee up to meet his nose. *Crunch*. The tips of her toes intersected with his balls as she dropped him.

His friends added a new set of notes when she eye-socket punched one of them and tripped the other onto the sidewalk and slammed his head off the ground a few times.

That pair limped off when she got to her feet. She dusted off her hands and turned to Jeoff, only to find him dragging the first dude by the foot.

Was he treating her like a damned lady again? "What are you doing? I said I would handle it."

"He was looking up your skirt." *Grrrr.* "I should eat his eyes."

Luna might have blinked at the rather violent suggestion. "I've heard that, while they might pop like grapes, they don't taste as good."

His turn to blink with long lashes as he tore his gaze from the cowering thug to her. "I don't even want to guess how you came by that information."

No, he probably didn't. But her observation did serve to distract him from cannibalism—which the authorities totally frowned upon. Dropping the thug, Jeoff strutted to the car, and this time, she didn't feel an urge to remind him that women had burned their bras for the right to open their own damned door. She let him open the door to the passenger side, just like she let him drive, but where she got annoyed was when he thought he'd just drop her off at the condo.

She crossed her arms over her chest. "I am not getting out until you agree to come up with me."

"I just want to go to bed."

"And you can. At my place. We're not done with our mission."

"What mission? We discovered absolutely nothing."

On the contrary, she knew Jeoff wanted her. That counted for something. "We haven't found a clue yet is what you should say. I still think we're on the right track. That club has something to do with what happened to those people. I can tell you, though, that we definitely won't get any insider info if it looks like we're not truly a couple. Or had you forgotten the targets are people in relationships? We need to keep up the guise."

"It's after eleven at night." Their club visit had been short-lived. "There's nobody to notice."

She snorted. "Maybe the puppies are good dogs who go to bed early. This is the pride, Jeoff. You should know better. There's always someone awake and watching. "

Jeoff sighed. Again. The poor man. She began to think he did it because he liked the sound, but at least he knew when to concede defeat. "Fine. I'll come up, but I am not sleeping over." He wagged his finger at her. "I'll stay an hour or so, long enough for them to think we did it, and then I'm leaving."

No, he wasn't, but he didn't need to know that yet.

He parked his precious car in her underground parking spot. It wasn't as if her bike would need it for a few days. Sob.

As if he read her mind, he laced his fingers in hers as they walked to the elevator and muttered, "Petrov is already working on it. You'll get your bike back good as new. And knowing Petrov, he'll have tweaked your performance."

She perked up. "Really? Sweet."

The elevator arrived immediately, opening doors onto an empty cab that they entered. A silence stretched between them as the elevator lurched into motion and immediately stopped at the lobby level floor.

Before the doors finished opening, she'd plastered her mouth over Jeoff's, feeling his gasp of surprise, loving how his mouth clung to hers. The man might protest, but deep down, he wanted it.

Wants me.

Rowr.

"Hey, girls, look. Luna brought home a pet."

Luna almost snarled at the interruption. The kiss that began as a decoy for anybody who might see them had quickly turned into an embrace that needed a few more minutes to get X-rated.

Hands yanked at her and Jeoff. Tugged into the lobby by Stacey, Luna waved at a few of her crew splayed on the couches. It seemed she wasn't the only one whose night had gotten cut short.

Joan sat up straight on the couch. "Holy shit. Luna was trying to sneak Jeoff up to her room."

Sneak? She wasn't the one ashamed of their fake relationship. Luna looped her arm in his. "Damned straight I was trying to sneak past. I knew you'd try and cock block me if you got a chance."

Jeoff choked. Poor thing. She knew the pain of hairballs in the throat.

"You are not sleeping with him. No way. I don't believe it." Melly shook her head. "You're not his type."

At that, several of her crew nodded. It made a girl want to prove them wrong. It made a wolf actually do it, and it started with him lowering his lips until they hovered but a whisker away.

Warm air tickled her lobe. "Are you going to gab with your girls all night, or are we going to your room?" Everyone heard the low rumble of his words, and not a single lioness missed the possessive placement of his hand on her ass.

"Bye, biatches!" Luna waved goodbye before she practically dragged Jeoff to the elevator. For good measure, she plastered her mouth to his before the doors closed and kept kissing him well after.

He finally came up for air when the elevator lurched into motion. "Good job keeping our cover."

"You mean that tongue wasn't for real?"

"Just keeping in character."

"Tease," she grumbled. For a second there, with the way he'd responded, she'd thought for sure he'd let his morals cave.

One night. Just one night is all we need to cure ourselves of this insane curiosity.

The thing she feared most? One night wouldn't be enough.

Keep him.

Her cat had no problem with the idea of hoarding him for selfish reasons. Luna didn't like what that implied.

Permanence. Ugh. What a nasty word.

The elevator dinged, telling her they'd arrived. As the doors opened, Jeoff level his gaze on her. "You really have to stop doing that."

"Doing what?"

"Thinking that things will go any further."

Way to read her mind. "I don't think. I know. You and I will end up in bed. Or in an alley somewhere. The place doesn't matter. We are going to do it." She smirked at him as she headed up the hall to her door. Only as she entered did she notice he didn't follow. She stuck her head out. Jeoff stood by the elevator still.

She whistled.

His eyes narrowed.

She whistled again and snapped her fingers. "Here, wolfie. Come to Luna for a nice belly rub."

"I really hate it when you do that."

"I really hate the way you keep getting me horny and not following through, so get your ass over here, would you?"

"You cannot just order me around. And I thought we'd already ascertained that the whole couple thing downstairs was for show, not for real."

She couldn't help but roll her eyes. "Maybe if you keep saying it, you'll believe it. But for the moment, it's pathetic the way you're lying. I can see it. Anyone can. You're hot for me, just like I'm hot for you. It is causing major distraction issues. Especially for me. So let's get it out of the way. Knock boots and ease the tension." She hummed a tune, the *bow-chica-wow-wow* harmony that invoked images of a thick seventies mustache on the repair guy at the door, which, of course, was answered by a lingerie-clad, buxom woman.

He didn't appreciate her ability to hit the right notes. He snapped. "And this is why I don't date lionesses. You're all fucking nuts." A very interesting bellow erupted from him as he shoved through the door that led to the stairs and disappeared.

Chase him.

Chase? Hell no. She let him walk away. That's right. *She let him* walk away instead of hunting him down. She was done forgoing her own pride because of her lust for him. It utterly disgusted her the way she kept throwing herself at him. Practically begging him to take her, only to have him say no and keep saying no, even though his body said yes.

The nerve. How the constant rejection stung.

We should totally rake our claws over him. Rip the clothes from him. Scratch that sweet, smooth skin.

Bad kitty. Those kinds of thoughts were the reason she got in trouble.

What the hell was wrong with her? Jeoff wasn't interested. Plain and simple. Why did she keep forcing the issue? Why?

Because I like him.

Ugh.

Like really liked him and it burned her to no ends that he didn't feel the same, which meant he left and she didn't go after him.

No chase? Her inner feline seemed most crushed, judging by the low slink back to her condo. She slapped her hand on the security screen alongside it again, the door having shut on its own and locked.

It clicked, and she swung the door open. The dark interior beckoned her, and she stepped in, alone, with a sigh.

There was no scent to warn her. No sound. Nothing.

And all she managed was a snarl before something jabbed her in the arm.

Chapter Ten

Don't go back. Don't go back.

The mantra kept him company for two flights down.

I should stay. Just for an hour. Can't let my emotions screw with our cover.

The excuse he used as he took the steps two at a time back up.

The hall for her floor was empty, and he didn't know the exact number of her place. As if he needed such a mundane detail. He knew with unerring accuracy which door belonged to her. Her scent—sweet hot grass in the summer with a hint of wildflower—lingered in the air and gave it away. He stopped in front of her door and tried the knob. It didn't turn, the door sealed against him.

Keeping us out. His wolf didn't like barriers. He wasn't crazy about it either.

An urgency possessed him, a need to get on the other side of that door. He pounded on it. "Luna, it's me. Open up."

Nothing.

Perhaps she sulked.

Danger.

The whispered warning from his wolf had no basis. No scent. No sound, and yet…

He pounded again and thought he heard furtive movement from within, but nothing else. It seemed so out of character. Luna never shied away from anything. She didn't own a timid bone in her luscious golden body. So why the utter silence?

Something is wrong.

The wrongness tainted the air, tugged on his sixth sense. Such an insistent pull that wanted him inside, now. But how?

The doors were equipped with deadbolts, and the doors sat in steel frames embedded in concrete walls. Add the lack of room in the hall and it made kicking or ramming it open less than feasible. He wouldn't get in this way unless someone opened the door or a key suddenly appeared.

I need another way in. It wasn't as if he could turn into a mouse and use air vents or fly like a bird up to her window.

Window. Thinking of them reminded him of the layout of the condos and their balconies.

A door a few feet over teased him. It belonged to the guest suite his sister had stayed in when she was having some troubles a while back.

I wonder if I still have access. A long shot, but… He slapped his hand on the scanner. The door clicked, and he was in, and hopefully not about to confront someone angry at his intrusion.

Nothing leaped at him. The room smelled stale, obviously not in use. Not that he cared. Jeoff ran across the living space to the sliding doors and flung them open so he could step out onto the balcony. A quick glance to his left showed the veranda next door for Luna.

What he didn't expect to see was some big dude wearing a hoodie pulled low over his face with Luna slung over his shoulder.

Who the fuck is he? Grrr. His wolf immediately

bristled, pushing hard enough at the line between them for him to pull his lip back in a snarl.

He dares to attack Luna?

Not on his watch. "Put her down." Jeoff vaulted to the lip of the balcony, balancing on the front part of his feet. He gauged the distance between the verandas. He could make it.

Hopefully.

If not... He peeked downward. *Yeah, let's try and not splat.*

He would have liked more time to think about the leap—to calculate the laws of physics and the chain of events that would lead to success, or failure—but the big dude wasn't obeying his request to put Luna down. He seemed to think he could just take her. As for Luna, she didn't fight; she hung limp and unmoving. It tightened his heart.

She better not be dead.

Jeoff didn't even want to contemplate that possibility.

The hooded dude stepped up onto the wide concrete lip of the balustrade. Only one way to go from there, and down was too many stories to survive.

Like fuck are you taking Luna with you on your suicide dive.

The muscles and tendons of his legs tightened. He sprang, extending himself forward, hands reaching for the other balcony. But gravity, a law nobody seemed to defy, wanted him badly. It pulled at his body, dragging his arching leap downward. His hands hit the rail for the other unit, his fingers grappling for purchase as his body slammed into the side and his legs dangled.

"Bastard!"

He might have felt more gratified at hearing

Luna rousing from her unconscious state if his fingers weren't holding on for dear life. Damned concrete abraded the tips. Ignoring the pain, he gritted his teeth and pulled himself up, galvanized by the grunts and snarls happening on the other side of the solid rail.

Pulling himself up high enough to rest on his forearms, he noted Luna in full lioness mode, growling and swiping at the big dude, whose hood hid his features. Even more disconcerting, Jeoff couldn't detect a scent.

He vaulted onto the balcony just as Luna lunged at the intruder, claws extended. Her lunge was off, and yet she still managed a swipe that tore fabric and sliced skin. A slow reaction time to recover meant she missed blocking the jab of the needle by her assailant, a big syringe that saw yellow liquid injected into her body.

In moments, the drug took effect, and Luna wavered on her four feet. Before the hooded fellow could take advantage of her, Jeoff hit the floor of the veranda and held out his bleeding fingers, beckoning. "Why not tangle with someone your own size, asshole?"

"Not tonight. But don't worry." The voice lowered. "I'll be back for her." The guy leaped onto the railing and waggled his fingers. Jeoff couldn't understand where he thought he'd go. As for the pissed and wobbly lioness, she didn't care about the lack of safety net. She swiped a paw tipped in claws. The fellow leaned backwards, almost managing a *Matrix*-type move. Almost. Gravity wanted him, though, and instead of fighting it, with wind-milling arms, the hooded dude extended them and fell backwards.

Holy shit.

Jeoff raced to the railing and peered downward, expecting to see guts splattered, only to utter a, "Fuck me, what the hell is that?" as something with dark wings burst free from its shirt and flew away.

"Rowr."

He peeked over at Luna, who had two furry paws on the ledge and wobbled. "The drugs trying to put you to sleep?"

"Rowr. Rowr. Rowr." He'd take that for a yes as she wobbled and sat down hard on her ass.

"Come on, let's get you inside." Since Luna seemed intent on sleeping where she was, he had to grab her, which, given she was currently a giant kitty, meant snagging her around the middle and carrying her legs dangling back inside. Then where to put her?

The couch was covered in crap. Books, video game controllers, an empty pizza box. The floor proved no better with the collection of socks, empty water bottles, and what might have been a glazed donut once stuck to the carpet.

"Someone needs a maid," he muttered as he lugged her limp body to the bedroom. There was one big bed that, while disheveled, was clear enough for him to drop her on.

Now what? He thought about calling a doctor, but Luna's breathing came easily, with a hint of a snore. Given it seemed most likely she'd been given a sleeping agent, he decided to keep his skin intact since she would probably ribbon it if he let someone examine her while she was vulnerable.

The fact that she was vulnerable brought home an important fact. Someone had attacked her. And hadn't just attacked her; they'd invaded what should have been a safe place.

Time to bring Arik up to speed. Shit was getting serious. The thugs outside the club wanting his car he could excuse as a crime of chance. It happened, especially in the less savory parts of town. But this? An attack on a pride member on pride turf?

The king of this concrete jungle needed to know, but Jeoff didn't look forward to the roar. Felines could be so noisy when threatened.

He left Luna, still wearing her jungle kitty, snoring in the bedroom, softly closing the door behind him. Standing in the messy living room, he tried to find signs of the intruder as he dialed Arik.

It took but two rings before the bossman answered in a sleepy voice. "This better be good. I've got an nine a.m. meeting with some douchebag—"

"Visiting dignitary from Europe," Kira interjected in the background.

"Whatever. I need sleep. So why are you calling?"

It took only a few minutes of explanation before a roar shook the condo, the sound reverberating through the ventilation shafts and tugging on the tenuous connection that existed with everyone in the pride. Even Jeoff was not immune. The king was pissed.

The king was also at the door to Luna's condo a short time later, not needing a key or permission to enter. He stalked in like he owned the place—which he technically did.

"Where is she?" Without waiting for an answer, Arik peeked in on Luna and grunted. "Must have been some good drugs. It's not easy to take her down."

"Must have been." Kneeling in the mess, Jeoff held up a syringe, only a portion of the fluid gone.

"She must have knocked it away when he tried the first time. That's probably why she revived for a bit on the balcony. But she got a full second dose. I'm going to guess she'll be out for hours."

"And she is going to wake up peeved." Arik made a grimace. "Not something I'm looking forward to."

A lioness on a rampage wasn't something anyone wanted to experience. "I'm surprised you came down. Given what happened, I would have thought you'd be practically sitting on Kira." Because given the brazen attack, surely Arik had some concern for the human he'd taken as mate.

"I dumped her on Leo and Meena. Nobody is getting through those two." Leo alone was a force to be reckoned with. Add his new mate and disaster was a surety.

"I don't know if we need to worry about them hitting us again tonight. Once the dude lost the element of surprise, he took off."

"Took off on wings. Dark ones, you said. But did I hear you right? He had no feathers?"

"No feathers." The recollection made no sense. The avian shifters all had feathers. All of them, and they also tended to be much finer boned. That big dude was a beast. How the hell did he fly—and keep a mostly manlike shape? When shifters took their animal form, there was nothing human left about them. But this fellow…

Jeoff shook his head. "I don't know what that guy was. I've never seen anything like him before."

"What of his scent?"

"Does spring-time fresh dryer sheet and deodorant count? If I hadn't seen the fucker fly away, he could have passed as human."

Arik paced, his expression thoughtful and worried. "I'll have to make some calls. Maybe someone in the other prides, clans, or packs have heard of this kind of thing."

"I'm going to go on the record and say I've never heard of it. But I'll make some calls too. Perhaps the Lycan council has records or something that might identify it."

"Report back what you find. Now, what of its purpose? Why did it come here? Why come after Luna?"

A part of Jeoff wondered if it had to do with their visit to the club that night. But that was jumping to assumptions. "We can't know he came specifically for her. It could be she just proved handy. I mean, if the dude can fly, he could have landed on any balcony and looked for an unlocked door."

The observation caused a furrow in Arik's brow. "This flying thing is disturbing. It means none of our homes are safe because I don't think anyone locks that damned patio door. Something that changes tonight. I'll have to put a warning out to the pride. I don't think we can hide what's happening anymore."

"Do you think it's connected?" Jeoff asked since Arik had decided to make the tenuous connection.

"Don't you?"

At this point, too many coincidences were piling up. "Whoever it is, they're acting pretty fucking brazen."

"Or they're looking to start a turf war." In the shifter world, there were always power games being played. "What about this Gaston Charlemagne, the one who owns the club you hit tonight? You didn't say much about him. What's the deal?"

Jeoff rolled his shoulders. "No deal. At least none that we could dig up. He practically doesn't exist, except on paper."

"Change that. I want to know more about this guy, starting with if he's shifter or human. If he is one of us, then he apparently needs a reminder that he's on my turf and needs to abide by my rules. If he's not, then check out his staff, see if any of them could be our culprit. I want answers."

"I'll hunt him down in the morning. As well as question the staff a little more officially." The time for subterfuge was at an end. Shit got serious with Luna's failed attack. Time to go at the possible source with teeth bared and claws out.

"Do it. Also, I'm going to want extra security for the pride."

"I can arrange that, but you do know the lionesses won't like it." They saw any form of security as babysitting.

"They will do as I say." Arik's eyes held a hard glint. "And I'm going to tell them that at the pride meeting I'm going to call. It's time I warned them of what's happening so they can be on the look out."

"What if we have a spy? You'll be tipping our hand."

"I think it's already tipped. And if there is someone stupid enough to think they can betray us, then we'll find them and take care of them."

The word permanently didn't need to be said. The implication was clear. "I'll get on it in the morning right after I run by my place for a change of clothes."

"Morning?" Arik arched a golden brow. "I didn't realize you were staying the night."

"Only so I can watch over Luna. She's out from the drugs and vulnerable. I thought I'd stick around, at least until she wakes up."

"Vulnerable?" Arik snickered. "If she wasn't asleep, she'd rake you over with her claws for that."

Fine with him. Jeoff wouldn't mind a little scratching action, with her. Wrong thought. He really needed to keep his distance from the temptation she posed, which was why he couldn't understand why he didn't take up Arik on his offer.

"You can go home if you like. I'll sit with her or get Hayder and Arabella to come over."

"Nope. Let them rest. I've got this."

Crazy talk, Jeoff thought as he shut the door behind Arik and secured it with a chair under the knob. The condo's fancy lock systems were all well and good, but electronics could be hacked. Old-fashioned methods, such as a wedge, never failed. Unless someone used a pickup truck and rammed at the blocked doorway. But that case was years ago, and he didn't see a truck being able to make it to her floor. Still, though, precautions should be taken.

Most likely, the flying dude had swooped down and entered through an unlocked balcony. Jeoff couldn't be one hundred percent sure because of the lack of scent for tracking. With nothing to smell, he relied on logic, especially knowing how hard it would be for a stranger, especially one with, oddly, no scent, to infiltrate the building and get in through the door. So he assumed the dude had come through the balcony, which was why he thumbed the latch. It wouldn't stop anyone determined to get in, but the snapping of it would give audible warning.

The sliding door wasn't the only point of entry. There was another window in the bedroom. *I should check it.*

Totally check it, his wolf too eagerly agreed.

No need to ask why. His shaggy other side liked being around Luna. Liked her smell. The touch of her hands on him. The taste of her lips. As a matter of fact, his wolf liked just about everything about her.

And so do I. It galled him to admit, but at the same time, hadn't this always been true? How many years since he'd first noticed Luna? Lusted after her, but done his best to ignore her? Now, circumstance had thrown them together, forced him to get close. Vey close. Problem was he now couldn't seem to get away.

Don't want to go away. His inner beast said it succinctly.

That attitude was a problem. But he'd have to suck it up and remind himself that he had promised Arik to watch over Luna. That meant going into that bedroom and checking on that damned window.

So why did he hesitate? He'd put her to bed all big and furry. Nothing to tempt him. Nothing to make him do something stupid.

The door opened quietly, and he poked his head in. Sucked in a hard breath. In her sleep, Luna had shifted, her tawny lioness pulled back to leave bared skin.

Stop staring!

He really shouldn't ogle, especially given her condition. The window still needed checking, though, which meant he had to go in.

Be brave.

He walked into the bedroom, keeping his gaze averted from the bed, skirting the foot of it to get to the other side to check on the window. It showed no signs of tampering, and the lock was firmly engaged.

He made to circle around the bed again, his intent being to escape to the living room, where he could fight the allure of her scent. Instead, he found himself stopping by the head of the bed and staring down at Luna. She lay splayed on her stomach again. Face angled to the side, lips parted and snoring softly. In the dim light, he could barely see the pattern of freckles across the bridge of her nose. The skin of her cheeks appeared smooth, alabaster perfection. He ran the backs of his knuckles against it, drawn to touch.

A soft sigh left her lips. So sweet.

Walk away. Don't stay in here. There was no reason to stay in here. He could make himself a spot on the couch.

Stay. She's vulnerable. No matter what Arik said, or she thought, Luna was currently defenseless. *I shouldn't go far.*

Also, that couch wasn't exactly built for a guy his size, and her bed was awfully big. The justifications convinced him to stay with her. The door proved easy to secure with another chair, leaving plenty of warning if someone chose to come crashing through. Unlike movies where heroes pulled an all-nighter keeping watch, he planned to catch some sleep because he couldn't deny the fatigue in his body. He would do nobody any good if he didn't get some rest.

Rationalization had him unbuttoning the top of his pants as well as stripping off his socks and his jacket. He removed his silken shirt in favor of donning his T-shirt, the one she'd borrowed from him lying on the foot of her bed. It held her scent within the cottony fibers. A pathetic excuse for a wolf, he sniffed it. And, no, he wouldn't hang his head in shame because no one knew but him.

Before getting into bed with her, with his eyes averted, he tucked the comforter to a spot under her chin, ensuring she was fully covered. Only then did he dare clamber onto the mattress, keeping to the far side, lying atop the covers, not touching her at all, yet so utterly aware of her.

What was it about Luna that made him want to forget all his promises to himself? How could one woman, one sensually sexy and frustration-inducing woman, make him want more than what they had? A part of him tired of keeping her at arm's length. He wanted to do more than lie beside her, pretending she wasn't inches away. Pretending he didn't yearn to hold her.

Show some respect. She was drugged, and despite all her invitations, she wouldn't appreciate him manhandling her. He used those arguments to lull himself to sleep, alone, on his side.

That was not how he woke up.

Chapter Eleven

Nothing beat waking up atop a guy, staring intently and waiting for him to rouse.

Unlike some of her previous sleepover friends, Jeoff didn't scream when he opened his eyes and spotted her. He also didn't smile. But, boy oh boy, was he rock hard underneath her.

She wiggled. "Morning, wolfie. I see someone is in the mood for a little something-something."

"Yup. A pee."

The man persisted in playing hard to get. "Is that what you're going with?" She tickled him in the kidney, trying to get a rise.

He stared.

"Oh come on, stop playing hard to get and admit you want me."

"I want you to get off."

"Gee, so do I, but someone won't help a girl out." She winked.

He still stared and tried to keep a cool expression, but his body couldn't hide his rousing heat.

"I take it you're feeling better?"

"If by better you mean awake." She grimaced. "Talk about an unfair fight. I never even smelled the bastard before he was jabbing me with a needle. Utterly mortifying."

"You obviously didn't make it easy for him. I

noticed he didn't get you entirely with the first dose."

She smiled. "A girl develops a sixth sense over time when it comes to guys putting on the moves. I wasn't expecting the needle, though. That's a new one. His drugs were good, but it's not the first time someone tried to roofie me. It's true what they say. Never put your drink down. The damned stuff made me slow. I tried to fight back." Her lips turned down. "He got me with a cuff to the head, which was why I got knocked out the first time."

She wondered if he even realized just how much concern his face showed at her words. His hand reached to cup the side of her head.

"How are you feeling now?"

"Refreshed and ready to go." To emphasize, she did a bit of a bounce.

He might have uttered a small, pained moan. "Stop that."

"No." She wiggled again until he stopped her with his hands on her hips, stilling her movements. "Ooh, getting physical. If you ask me, I totally deserve a spanking for that."

"You are not supposed to ask for a spanking."

"Why not?"

"It has to be spontaneous."

"I will get you to spank me one day," she threatened.

"Probably. But in the meantime, you'll just have to anticipate it." He slapped her on the butt and winked, his abrupt swap from scowl to teasing grin jarring. The bloody man blew hot and cold and freaking purple. Seriously. She really didn't know what to expect from him.

Which is why he's so much fun.

The saucy retort he made deserved a reply, yet

before she could utter something snazzy or scathing, Luna found herself gaping at her ceiling as Jeoff flipped her onto her back. He sprang out of bed, his dress pants of the night before hanging off the tight upper curve of his ass. Stupid gentleman wearing his clothes to bed. Even more horrid, the damned pants insisted on clinging instead of tumbling downward and flashing his sweet ass.

"Where are you going?" she couldn't help but ask. What she really wanted to say was "get your butt back over here." She was totally in a mood to maul him.

Apparently, he had different plans.

A chair set under the doorknob got more attention than she did. He removed it and set it to the side before opening the door, but he paused before exiting, finally deigning to reply. "First, I'm going for a pee. Followed by food. Then I need to hit my place for clothing before I go back to Rainforest Menagerie for a peek around. After that, I intend to stalk Charlemagne down."

"I? What happened to 'we'?" She set her lips in a stubborn line. "You are not going without me."

"Then be ready to go in the next ten minutes."

"Ten minutes?"

He smirked at her from the door of her room. "Yes, ten minutes if you're planning to come with me. I don't have time for girl nonsense. Arik's tasked me with getting answers, and that's what I'm going to do."

"Not alone you're not because I'm coming with you," she muttered as she hopped out of bed. If he thought she was one of those girls who took an hour to get ready, then he'd quickly learn.

Problem was he got a head start since he used her only bathroom to pee. The lock needed only a butter knife to pop it, and she entered the washroom, which caused him to yell, "What the fuck," and halt his pee mid-stream. Impressive control.

"Hey, wolfie." She sauntered in clad in absolutely nothing.

He kept his eyes on her forehead. "Don't hey me. I locked the door for a reason. It's called privacy."

"I don't know that word."

"Don't start with me, Luna. Couldn't you wait until I was done?"

"Nope. I'm on a deadline that I would like to point out you set. But don't mind me," she said with a naughty grin as she stopped behind him and peered around his body. "Go ahead and finish your pee while I get going on my shower."

Not surprisingly, he didn't finish his business and kept his hand cupped over his junk.

Point. Stepping past him, she lifted her foot over the rim of the tub and stepped in. Leaning, she stretched forward to turn on the water and then jerked back so the initial cold jet didn't get her. Since there was no shower curtain, the glass barrier that acted as splashguard gave her a perfect view of Jeoff, still standing in front of the toilet, head craned to gape at her.

She waved and smiled. "Why don't you join me?"

Glare, heated glare, and a tense posture.

Good. It wouldn't hurt him to feel some of her annoyance.

Men, not the pride males because they learned early on not to mess with lionesses, but other men, other kinds of shifters, always thought they could control situations. Thought a woman should be demure and seen, not heard. Screw that. Luna had always been a bit of a free spirit and a tomboy.

Aunt Zelda often lamented, *"June, how can you let her run wild?"* To which her darling mother replied, *"That's not wild. It's strength and character."*

What it meant was Luna didn't feel a need to bow to the status quo. She acted how she wanted, which, at times, proved a little outrageous. Most guys couldn't handle it. There was a reason Luna had a string of ex-boyfriends. It wasn't that she screwed them and left them, more a case of they couldn't handle her. Couldn't handle the fact that she wasn't fragile and dainty. She didn't cater to their egos. Didn't need them fighting her battles. She also interrupted them while they peed.

But, she should add, she didn't have a problem peeing herself in front of a guy. Not her fault they acted like it was a big deal when she had to pop a squat on a hike in the woods. They were just jealous her aim was more refined than theirs. For those that wondered, how good was her control? She could totally write her name, in cursive.

What she found interesting was, despite being herself, Jeoff hadn't yet run. Sure, he'd rebuffed her, but it was words. Just words. His actions were much more telling, and she didn't just refer to his almost constant hard-on when she was around him.

Jeoff spent the night. Spent it here with her because he was worried. He didn't have to. He could have easily called someone. Anyone in the pride would have come and guarded her snoring ass. But Jeoff didn't find a replacement. He chose to guard her himself, and she woke to find herself on his chest, his heart under her ear and his arms looped around her. Since she'd never slept with anyone like this before, she could assume only that he'd initiated the snuggle.

He'd snuggled her all night and now was trying to pull Mr. Prissy with her.

She had no sympathy for him. "So are you going to finish that pee?" she asked, lifting her face to the spray.

"No." While he might not be doing a number one, he also wasn't leaving. Nor was he properly staring, even though she wiggled her body under the spray.

He stood there, gaze unfocused, a puzzled frown creasing his brow.

Pivoting in the shower, she bent over to grab her all-in-one body wash. It didn't take long to lather herself head to toe. The entire time he watched, yet she couldn't have said if he even realized it, his attention obviously elsewhere.

Only when she was fully rinsed and the water turned off did he snap out of his fugue. He grabbed a towel from the bar on the wall and thrust it at her before turning on his heel and returning to her bedroom. She grabbed her toothbrush, tossed a dab of paste on it, and followed.

She scrubbed at her teeth as Jeoff stripped his T-shirt, showing off his awesome abs, perfect covered in smooth skin—the only improvement would have been teeth marks. He threaded his arms through the sleeves of his shirt from the previous night as she chewed on the bristles of her toothbrush and, one-handed, pulled out clothes of her own.

To slow him down, she dropped the towel and did her best to keep his attention. She succeeded pretty well given she hopped on a foot to get her undies on, began to froth at the mouth with toothpaste, and had wet hair plastered to her face.

Way to seduce him. Then again, this was the real

Luna. She didn't believe in artifice. *Which might be why I'm still single.* Still, she couldn't see herself playing some of the games she knew the other ladies did. She wasn't into makeup or the whole hair styling for an hour each day thing. She was a scrub her blonde mop top with a towel, twist it into a bun, and jam a clip into it kind of chick. She wore a bra, only so her boobs wouldn't bounce if she had to run, underwear under her jeans so the fabric wouldn't chafe, and an awesome T-shirt that had a pair of owls over each breast and stated, "Stop looking at my hooters."

Of course that never worked.

Jeoff stared. "Do you own any non-offensive shirts?"

She peeked in her open drawer. Shook her head. "Nope."

"Well, you can't wear that. Not if you want to come with me to hunt down Charlemagne."

"Are you seriously telling me what I can wear?"

"Yes."

Her gaze narrowed. "Make me." A fine challenge that had her light with anticipation.

So what did Jeoff do?

Turned on his heel and walked away. Would he leave? He had last night. What if he did again? She couldn't let him go off on his own. The damned man made her chase him.

"Where are you going?" she snapped at his back.

"I said you had ten minutes. You're not ready, so I'm leaving."

"I am too ready."

"Not in that shirt you aren't."

"You're a fucking prude, wolfie," she snarled.

"I'm okay with that," he hollered back. "Have

a great day." *Slam*.

The damned guy had left. "Oooh, sometimes I could strangle him," she grumbled as she darted into her closet and got out one of the dreaded *nice shirts* her Aunt Zelda had gotten for her. It was long sleeved, only slightly fitted, and covered in some girly flowery pattern. It went over the T-shirt since she didn't have time to waste.

She caught up to Jeoff as he was waiting for the elevator. He leaned against the wall, looking deliciously disheveled, his jaw sporting a rugged shadow, his hair rumpled.

He arched a brow. "You made it." He stepped into the open cab, and she followed.

"Of course I made it," she grumbled as she stabbed the button for the lobby.

"We need to get my car," he said as he pressed the one for the parking garage.

"We'll get there, but first…" The elevator doors slid open onto a lobby with a few lounging lionesses. "If you're going to make me wear something respectable, then that deserves payback, wolfie. Welcome to the walk of shame."

Given his whole stance on the not-getting-involved thing, she totally expected him to balk. But Jeoff kept surprising her. She couldn't help a spurt of irritation and interest as he slung an arm around her waist and, with a casual ease, strutted into the open with Luna. "Top of the morning, ladies."

The polite moniker had a few of them snickering.

"Looks like someone had a sleepover," Stacey remarked as she hugged her coffee with two hands and a hunch that said she'd had a good night.

"Who says we slept?" Jeoff uttered a wicked

chuckle that did really inappropriate things to Luna's nether regions. Now if only he'd follow through with the tease.

Two could play the teasing game, though. She dropped a hand to cup his butt. "Maybe next time, I'll let you be on top."

"Why do that when you were so happy to do all the work, kitten?"

He'd said it. The one word that Luna hated the most. The one that drove her feminine side ballistic. Before she could bite his tongue off, his lips were on hers. He kissed Luna and her anger melted, even amidst the comments.

"I can't believe she didn't kill him for that."

"Damn, they kinda make me want to get a dog of my own."

"Get a room. With a video camera set up for live streaming."

Breathless and addled—probably a lingering effect from the drugs—they made it out of the lobby alive, if horny.

Spilling into the parking garage, she was a few steps slower and behind Jeoff as he strutted to his wheels. How dare he look so unaffected by the kiss? It wasn't fair.

Over and over, he kept blowing mixed signals. Kept teasing her. Making her think she had him and then yanking the silky sheets out from under her. The frustration she felt? His fault. Everything annoying her in that moment was his fault. And he dared to strut.

She pounced on him, uttering a growl as she leaped. She wanted to hurt him in that moment. Take him down to the ground and pummel him a few times. At least she meant to. He whirled at the last second, caught her mid-air, and drew her against him.

"Is there a problem?"

"Yes there's a problem," she snapped. "You are a tease."

"And you're not?"

"I wouldn't be if you just let go for a stupid minute. Then we could get this whole sexual tension thing out of the way."

"You really think once will quench it?" His hands cupped her ass, pushing her against him, putting in blatant evidence of his erection. "What if we let go, as you say, and it's not enough? What if you want more? What if I want more?"

She gaped at him. "Are you talking about dating?"

"Yes, dating. A commitment to each other."

"Are you talking about a real relationship?" Her nose wrinkled, and she pushed away from him. "Hold on a second there. Who said anything about this being more than sex? You need to slow down there, wolfie."

"Are you seriously accusing me of going too fast? You're the one who keeps pushing me to drop my pants and perform."

"Well, yeah, I am, because sex is easy. You get naked, you screw, it's done. What you're suggesting…" She made a moue. "That never ends well." She had a track record to prove it too.

"Exactly. At least we both understand that it wouldn't end well. And this is why there will be no sex."

"Because you're afraid you'll fall for me?" The idea seemed too impossible to contemplate, yet he seemed completely serious.

"Very afraid. And I don't think either of us want that."

He was right. Totally right. Think of it, she and the wolf a real couple? What a joke. It would never work. Cats and dogs didn't belong together.

It works for Arabella and Hayder.

Because they were meant for each other. Whereas she and Jeoff weren't. Right? Right?

She mentally queried, but her inner lioness wouldn't answer.

It was enough to keep her quiet for the ride over to his place, where they spent only a few minutes as Jeoff changed from scruffy sleepover partner into slick dude in a suit with those ridiculously sexy glasses.

Rowr.

The car ride over to the club from his place wouldn't take long, which meant she didn't have much time to erase the weird tension between them. "So, now that you've had a chance to think it over, wanna fuck?" She punctuated it with a squeeze of his thigh.

He sighed. "Are we going to have this talk again?"

"Yes, because you seem to have this impression you'll fall for me and be stuck with me as your mate for life." Which totally scared the panties off her too. "But ask any of my ex-boyfriends, and they'll tell you I am not girlfriend material."

"Because they're idiots."

"Excuse me?"

"The fact they couldn't handle you means shit."

"Is this your way of saying you can handle me?"

Taking his gaze from the road, he tossed her a look that said, *"Duh."*

She sighed. "It's a shame you're not a lion."

"If I were a lion, we wouldn't be having this

conversation."

"What would we be doing instead?"

No reply, just the grasp of her hand on this thigh and sliding it over his groin. Once again, sending mixed signals. And he wondered why she kept trying to get in his pants.

Since he seemed determined to keep her off balance, she changed the subject. "So what do you think? Is this Charlemagne guy some sort of nefarious mastermind? Is he kidnapping shifters to do dastardly things?"

"No idea, but given what happened at his club last night, there's something afoot. Something is going on, and I want to find out what."

"I still don't understand why they doused the room with the drug. It made no sense at all."

"Beats me why they'd do it. Maybe it was a stunt to make news of this club go viral."

"But that kind of news is the type that would bring cops poking around. A club already skirting the edge of a few laws is one thing; a giant orgy is another. Even the cops can't turn a blind eye to that. And while I'm not a businessman, I can't see a smart one wanting that kind of attention."

"Assuming he's smart."

"True." Her fingers drummed the armrest on the door. "Since you can't find any address for this Charlemagne guy, other than the club, how are you going to find him?"

"I'm hoping we can squeeze an employee or two for info."

"At this time of the morning?"

"After last night's mess, they're going to have to do cleanup."

"Speaking of cleanup, we need to eat."

"How does cleaning make you think of your stomach?"

"Because I like to clean off the plate." She mimed a long lick.

Groan. "Stop it."

"Make me. Or, even better, punish me."

He didn't. Instead, he hit a fast food restaurant drive-thru and ordered some breakfast sandwiches and juice.

"No coffee?" She wrinkled her nose.

"You of all people don't need caffeine."

"No caffeine?" she gasped. "Isn't that cruelty to cats?"

"Swinging you by the tail is cruel. This is being honest."

"Honesty would be you just giving in to the inevitable. It will happen," she threatened as she got out of the car, her running shoes hitting firm asphalt.

Take that, evil grate. There would be no footwear malfunction today.

Without the crowd waiting to get in the club, and it being a Sunday, the road was pretty quiet, especially this time of the day. A few stray cars and trucks hummed along the road. A person in loose khakis and an oversized lumber jacket meandered along the sidewalk on the other side, head bopping to some tunes.

The outside of the club looked less than impressive in daylight, the neon sign dark, the exterior surface of the building painted a matte black. The previous evening, ground-level strobe lights painted it with brilliance and gave it a dazzling aspect. Exciting and pulse-pounding at night, kind of sad and in need of color in stark daylight.

The front doors, a metal set with riveted seams

and sturdy metal handles, were locked, a chain and padlock running through the loops.

"I don't think anyone's here," she stated, giving it a yank and hearing it clang as it fell back against the door.

"Not anyone who came through the front," he observed. A furrow creased his brow. "Which is odd. I mean, the place got doused last night. You'd think he'd have a cleaning crew of some sort in there, and yet I don't see any trucks or cars parked nearby."

She'd not even thought to look.

Some predator you are.

Hey, you didn't tell me to check either.

Her cat gave a mental sniff and turned away.

Saucy thing. Still, though, she really should pay more attention. Things had gotten serious the previous night with that guy trying to nab her. What the hell was that about? She was pretty damned glad Jeoff had returned for her.

He saved us. We should reward him. The kind of licking suggested didn't have anything to do with grooming.

"We should check the alley and the back of this place. Maybe they didn't come in this way."

A trek around the warehouse didn't reveal any unlocked doors; the one they'd come out of the previous night was shut tight. The one-way road running through the back was busy with delivery trucks, but no one else. By all indications, the place appeared abandoned. Odd because, as Jeoff said, after the water damage of the previous night, surely they would have cleaners in bright and early in order to prep the space for reopening as soon as possible.

Returning to the front of the building, they both leaned against his car—carefully so as to not scratch it and close enough to stroke it—and stared at the locked club.

"So now what, wolfie? There goes our plan to question someone who works here."

"Perhaps that's for the best."

"What do you mean?" she asked, following him around to the trunk of his car. He popped it and leaned in, pulling out a set of bolt cutters.

"It's best because whoever we questioned probably would have lied. People who do shit they shouldn't always do."

"I do stuff I shouldn't, but I don't lie about it."

He placed the bolt cutters on the chain. "No, you tell the truth, which is, at times, even scarier."

"Are you scared of the truth?"

He stared her straight in the eye. "Yes. Very much so."

Funny because the truth frightened her too. A lot of things Jeoff said scared the bejesus out of her. Especially the truth where he feared once together wouldn't be enough.

So we have sex two or three times. At one point, they'd get bored. Jeoff would realize she wouldn't ever be dainty or girly. He'd want someone who wouldn't think it was fun to randomly arm wrestle for the remote. Who wouldn't flush the toilet while he was in the shower on purpose just to hear a scream.

Eventually, the things Luna did would get to him. *I'd drive him crazy. He'll leave.* Or she'd see it coming and take off first. Once a guy cried because she beat him every single time they raced on his game system, there was no going back.

But what if Jeoff didn't leave? What if he stuck around? And she stuck around. And they became...

Snick. The cutters sliced through the metal link

of the chain, drawing her attention. Another clip separated it completely.

"This is breaking and entering." Given she recognized a crime in progress, she felt a need to mention it.

"Are you uncomfortable with bending certain human laws?"

"No." It made her panties wet.

He took a moment to glance both ways. Seeing no one, he pulled the noisy thread of metal through the handles. "Since the place is empty and we can't question anyone, I've got a better way of getting information."

He stuffed the lock and chain in the trunk of his car, along with the bolt cutters. Before slamming it shut, he reached in to grab a small tool kit. He pulled open his coat and tucked it into his inner pocket.

She grabbed the edge of his jacket before it fell back into place.

"What's that for?" That being the gun sitting in the holster strapped around his body. It surprised her. Luna was more of a hands-on kind of girl. "Isn't that a touch unsporting?" She preferred a paws-on approach herself.

"I call it evening the odds and making sure I don't push up daisies. I intend to be prepared in case we run in to bat dude again."

"Bat dude? Is that what you're calling it?" Her nose wrinkled at the very idea. "I've never heard of one."

"Me either. But then again, how much does the shifter community really get together and talk about who they are? We are a secretive bunch. For all we know, there are moose shifters or caribou ones up in the North."

"Beaver ones too!"

"Okay, now you're just being silly."

"Says the guy who is talking about a bat."

"Well, what else do you want me to say? It's what it mostly resembled."

"Says you. I think it looked like—" Her fuzzy mind rewound to the previous night, pushing for an image. She got one; a giant mouse with wings. "You know what. It doesn't matter what it looks like. The point is you have a gun."

"I do."

"And I don't."

"Which is probably safer for the world at large."

She stomped his foot and hip checked him out of the way, not because of his rude remark—okay, maybe a little—but mostly because she wanted inside first.

Some men would bellow or rail or sulk—the worst—but Jeoff gave her sarcasm. "Ladies first."

She gave him a finger because she wasn't a lady, as she fought a grin because he'd called her one.

Her back to him, she took a moment to look around. Not much to see. Just a small inner chamber with the bench from last night where she'd filled out that stupid form.

How many times a week do you masturbate for your partner?

None, because she preferred to torture herself.

Since she doubted any secrets were hidden in what amounted to the mudroom of the club, she yanked at the second set of doors. They held. Another lock.

"Hey, wolfie. Got a bobby pin?"

"Lock picking is a pain in the ass." He ran his

hands over the door, checking it out. Then he took a few steps back and raised his foot.

Bang. The thick sole of his boot hit the door, and something cracked. The door popped open, another dead bolt shot.

In the silence right after, they both stood still and listened. If someone was in the building, they'd have heard. They held their breaths and tongues as they listened.

Nothing.

"I'd say we're clear. After you." He swept a grand gesture.

"You go first." She repeated his gesture and smiled.

"Are you using me as a shield in case someone has a gun trained on us right now?"

She blinked with false innocence and pointed to herself. "Who, me?"

He laughed and stepped in, not once flinching or pausing. A wolf with the balls of a lion.

Rowr.

Entering the vestibule quickly behind him, Luna was struck by yet more disappointing change. Last night, with the soft lighting and thrumming music, the room seemed such an exotic place. The muted glow of scattered lights had given the space an otherworldly feel.

In the glare of daylight streaming through the door, the rose-colored goggles were gone, leaving the unvarnished truth. She noted the lumpy concrete floor, painted a deep red, scuffed by heels and shoe soles. What she took for a starlit sky was actually sound-proofing panels bolted to the wall and painted a flat black. Metallic stickers in the shapes of stars were sprinkled across them.

It looked tacky, just like the bar itself. She entered the first cavernous chamber and couldn't help but note it appeared less than impressive. Last night the long bar oozed space-age cool with its glass top lit up from underneath so that it appeared to float. Changing lights aimed from above painted the concrete floor in colorful patterns. Even the shadows courtesy of dim lights over each of the doors didn't hide the scuffed flooring still damp in spots from the shower the night before.

She wondered if the lack of windows and air in this place was the reason for the musty smell. It didn't smell of heat, people, and sex—hot, adrenalized sex— not anymore.

"Hard to believe this is the same place. It's so…dull."

"It's the reality."

Reality sucked.

She peeked around and realized something was missing. The room seemed emptier somehow, and she didn't mean just people emptier. This was the area with couches, and she found it interesting to note them gone. "I see they did some cleanup. I guess the furniture didn't survive the water."

"I hope they burned them after last night. The things people were doing on them." He shuddered.

"Nothing wrong with having sex," she answered, stepping into the center of the room to give herself a panoramic view.

"It was wrong. And I don't mean the sex part. I mean the part where those people started just going at it without control, and not necessarily with the people they should have done it with."

"Is this your way of saying you wanted to make out with someone else?" Jealousy, sheath thy claws!

"No. I'm glad it was you and not anyone else. And a good thing no one accosted you. I would have had a hard time hiding the body."

"Why would you have to hide a body?"

"Never mind. What I was trying to say is some things should only be done in privacy for the right reasons."

"Because you're a prude."

Sigh. "Fine. Yes. I'm a prude, and dammit, I won't apologize for it."

She tossed him a grin. "Good, because you shouldn't. It is frustrating, but cute."

Turning her gaze away from him, she rotated her inspection to the ceiling. It loomed high overhead, the metal structural beams strung with disco balls and thick wiring.

"Hard to believe this is the hottest club right now."

"Amazing what a lack of lighting and alcohol can do. Now we should get searching before our luck runs out and someone shows up."

"Where should we look first? I doubt there's anything out in the open. Personal files and stuff would need somewhere more secure."

"Agreed. There's got to be an office around here somewhere."

Indeed there was, overlooking the whole club on a second floor. The door to it took only a firm shove to open. Inside, the space remained dry, obviously on a separate zone than the other part of the club.

They went through drawers, sifting through the papers found there, mostly orders for alcohol, time sheets for employees, and other detritus relating to the running of a club.

No secret agendas involving the trafficking of shifters. No secret compartment in the drawer with hidden USB sticks containing digital snuff movies. Not even any handcuffs. The desk and filing cabinet weren't the only place they struck out. The computer locked them out after three invalid passwords, douchenozzle, Lunaisdaddomb, and lovemonkey not being correct.

And no, those weren't her passwords. Anymore.

They didn't find a single clue, other than the fact that the tequila wasn't from Mexico. The horror.

Skipping back down the stairs, she couldn't help but return to the dance floor, something nagging at her. Of the fairy dust the night before, not a trace seemed to remain, washed away most likely by the water.

Everything was washed clean, even all scent. So why did she feel they'd missed something?

Hidden. Her feline hinted at something, but what? There wasn't really much to see in this place. A vestibule, the main party areas, a storage area behind the bar with a washroom for employees and a place to hang. DJ booth, enclosed and kept dry from the deluge. What had they missed?

"Care to explain to me why you're trespassing?"

The sudden query startled a yell from both of them. And no wonder. Apparently, they'd both missed the guy who'd snuck up on them.

Chapter Twelve

The most emasculating thing that could happen to a hunter, other than someone shaving his fur while he slept? Someone sneaking up on him.

As in he did not notice. At all.

Wolf fail.

Whine.

It didn't matter Luna appeared just as surprised. How fucking embarrassing, especially since he yelped like a little startled pup.

Instinct took over, screaming danger. Whirling, Jeoff took quick stock of the stranger who walked more quietly than a spider on the ceiling, which, according to his sister, was false. She claimed the distinct click of their eight legs always made a noise. She would know since she screamed bloody murder every time he'd let his hairy tarantula loose in her room when they were kids.

He'd grown more mature since then, which was why he didn't understand why he suddenly felt like a little boy in the presence of something big, so big that his wolf wondered if they should show their belly.

Excuse me? Like fuck.

The disturbing urge to submit made no sense. It wasn't as if the male he faced presented a clear and present danger. As a matter of fact, he didn't look like it would take much to take him down.

A lean dude, probably an inch or two over six feet. Black hair, with hints of red, slicked back, pale features, a thin nose and piercing eyes that looked less than impressed. The stranger held no weapon and didn't have the bulky build of a bruiser. Still, there was something that didn't sit right.

A low growl rumbled past his lips as his wolf bristled within, not liking the stranger at all. He took a deep breath for more clues, and it was then he understood his inner beast's agitation. Whoever this guy was, he didn't bear a scent apart from the fabric softener used on his smoky-gray Henley shirt.

Just like the guy last night. Except, this guy wasn't the right size. More than one fellow without a natural scent? That was something of concern, as was the battle for dominance occurring right now.

Eyes locked, they did a silent posturing dance. When males met for the first time, animal or human, it didn't matter. A certain posturing occurred as each man took the measure of the other. A glance up and down. A hitching of thumbs in belt loops. A hint of a disdain around the lips. It was part of establishing who was the more dominant one. Turned out it was Luna.

"Oh give me a break. You can both stop staring at each other. We all know who's the one in charge here." A pair of eyes swiveled her way, in time to catch her smirk. "Don't make me show you."

"Is she always so brazen?" asked the dude.

"*She* is right here. And *she* wants to know who you are," she uttered with the haughty disdain of a queen.

A brow arched. "Who I am? I believe I asked first, and unlike you, I have a right to be here. So, who are you, and why are you trespassing?"

"We're investigating what happened last night."

Jeoff had a ready answer.

"You are? Yet on whose behalf?" The man tapped his chin. "You're not cops. Cops need a warrant to enter without permission. And why would the police return when they left more than satisfied it was a patron who accidentally set off the alarm. You're most certainly not with the insurance company, since I didn't call them. So who does that leave?" He fixed a dark stare on them, a strangely compelling gaze that made Jeoff want to blurt all his secrets.

Yeah, no. Jeoff clamped his lips and stared right back. The man let a hint of a smile curve his lips before turning his mighty glare on Luna. Jeoff almost laughed. As if something like that would intimidate her.

Fists planted on her hips, she stared right back. "You might as well concede now. I don't blink. And, besides, I thought we already decided who was in charge here," Luna retorted.

The man sighed. "Damned animals. Your kind are always such a pain to deal with."

"Excuse me?" Jeoff said.

Head tilted at an angle, Luna perused the fellow more closely. "You know what we are, don't you?"

"A lioness and a wolf, meddling in my affairs. However did I get so lucky?" The sarcasm dripped.

"You got lucky because you forgot to report to the city's king." Continued perusal and sniffing of the guy still didn't let Jeoff identify the fellow. Strange, so fucking strange, because he'd never come across a person with no scent other than that of detergent on his clothes. Every living creature had a unique bouquet all their own, until now.

"You want me to report to your king?" Rich

laughter left a chill on the skin. "Why would I do that? Those rules apply only to your kind. As for me, I don't report to animals." Clear disdain hued his words.

More and more things didn't add up. "What are you?" Because the way the man spoke, his very attitude and apparent knowledge, made him more than human, but if he wasn't shifter, what was he? Contrary to popular belief, just because Lycans and other shapeshifters existed didn't mean a pantheon of other fairy tale creatures did. Or so Jeoff had been taught.

"I am none of your business."

Funny how those words seem to echo, teasing the edges of his mind, repeating over and over, a whispery mantra. He brushed it aside. "I'm making it my business." The words growled from him, and he leaned forward, the posture one of looming menace.

The fellow remained undaunted, standing his ground. "Do you really think you can force me?"

"Maybe he can't, but I can. Tell us. Now. Who are you?" Luna pressed closer, invading the guy's space, but he still didn't retreat and kept his cool expression as she paced around him. That took balls. A lioness on the prowl wasn't something to trifle with.

"Such interest in who I am. Then again, I guess there is no harm in announcing it. After all, I do plan to reside here for the foreseeable future. I am Gaston Charlemagne. The owner of Rainforest Menagerie, the club we are conversing in. As I am the proprietor, you will tell me why you broke in."

"What if we don't?"

"Then perhaps I shall allow the authorities to question you instead."

"Surely we can settle things as adults." Because the last thing Jeoff wanted was to bring the police in on possible shifter business. Luna already had enough strikes against her, but that didn't mean she knew when to hold her tongue.

"Settle things like an adult?" She uttered a snorted. "Speak for yourself. I say we pin his ass to the floor and start torturing him for answers."

"Tsk. Tsk." Charlemagne shook his head. "Animals. Always thinking violence is the answer. And so unnecessary, especially considering I have nothing to hide."

"If you have nothing to hide, then there is no harm in you maybe answering a few questions." Jeoff tossed the suggestion.

"If it will get you to leave, then ask."

"What do you know about the couples who have gone missing from your club?"

"People missing? That is the first I've heard of it. Are you sure you have the right location?"

Usually a good judge of character, Jeoff couldn't read the man. With no scent or body language to hone in on, he could only take his words at face value. "They all came here. And haven't been since." A stretch of the truth to see if he could startle a reaction.

Charlemagne didn't bat an eye. He replied with a slight shake of his head. "Why are you lying? Are you sure these people even came here, or are you fishing for information?"

How did the bastard know?

"Do you recognize these people?" Luna pulled out her phone and flashed some images saved on it.

One after another, Charlemagne shook his head. "Your persistence is commendable but misplaced. I do not personally greet all those who pass through my doors. They might have been patrons. They might not. I'm afraid I can't help you, and I wonder what you thought you would find by breaking into my club."

"We were looking for clues," Luna boldly stated.

"Did you find any? Perhaps some blood in the bathroom? A souvenir in the office? A body in the basement?"

"This place has a basement?"

"A small one for utilities, and not the point. Your search is unfounded and illegal."

"What's illegal is what happened here last night. We were here. We saw what happened." More like felt. The thing was, the drugs were gone, and his desire for Luna remained. Hell, it had existed before the drug too. Short of giving in, he wasn't sure he'd ever quite shake it.

"Were you looking for reimbursement because someone cut your evening short by setting off our sprinklers?"

"I'm looking to find out why everyone in the club was drugged."

At that accusation, Charlemagne's lips split as he let out a loud laugh. "Drugged? And what makes you think such a foolish thing?"

Again, Luna didn't couch her words. "The whole place turned into a giant orgy."

"Yes, I heard the patrons got friskier than usual the previous evening. What of it?" A supercilious raised brow went well with his reply.

"It was drug-induced," Jeoff accused, because how else to explain the loss of control that had almost led to him taking Luna on the floor, like an animal?

"That accusation is groundless. People got inspired and let their inhibitions down. You got caught up in it, a sexual version of mob mentality. Now you regret your actions and want someone to blame." His dark eyes glittered. "Nothing happened here last night. And nothing happened to those missing people. Unless you are actually with law enforcement with a warrant, I will ask that you leave. I am done answering your questions. The exit is that way." The man pointed, and Jeoff bristled. It was one thing to take orders from Arik, quite another from this upstart who thought himself above him.

As for Luna, no surprise, she didn't intend to listen. "You can stop with the orders. I am not done with you."

"Yes. You. Are. *Sleep.*" The fellow's hand rose, and he blew the dust sitting in the palm. Jeoff held his breath, determined to not inhale, but the fine particles still stung his eyes and settled on his skin.

In one blink of an eye to the next, he found himself outside on the sidewalk, sitting slumped, Luna at his side. "What the fuck just happened?" Jeoff asked as he jumped to his feet.

Luna darted forward and yanked on the door, yet despite the handles not being chained, it didn't move. Something secured it from inside. "How did we get here?"

I don't know. An emasculating admission he couldn't make. "I think that dude inside did something to us. Drugged us somehow with that powder he blew and then brought us outside."

"So I didn't just imagine what happened?" She cast him a glance. "You saw and talked to him too?"

"I did. And I've got to say I didn't like him at all."

"What the hell was he?" she asked as she stepped away from the door. Head craned back, she peered upward at the shuttered building, the windows all painted, none offering a glimpse of the inside, even if they could reach them.

"Fuck if I know what he was." He shrugged. "I was kind of hoping you would know."

"Nope. But he's obviously not human."

On that they could both agree. "Think he's here all alone?" If the guy didn't have backup, then perhaps they could storm the place and…what? He had no grounds for attacking the fellow. But they obviously couldn't ignore Charlemagne.

She tapped her bottom lip, her gaze distant. "He's strong, whatever he is, or at least wily. As for backup, I think he's got at least one, maybe more, of his kind with him. His lack of real body odor made me think of those bouncers last night. The one at the door and the one I clobbered. Not to mention the guy who jumped me in my apartment."

"What of our fellow in the woods?"

She rolled her shoulders. "Could be one of the ones we've met, or a new one. With no scent, I can't be sure. What I do know is there're too many of them, and I don't like it. We need to get back in there," she observed.

"Somehow, I don't think Charlemagne is going to answer if we knock."

"So we don't knock." She smirked. "We'll come back tonight and wait for the doors to open. He can't stop us from having a good time in his club."

Except, apparently, he could.

Despite the water mishap the day before, the club was open that night, busier than ever. But that wasn't the reason the bouncer, the same one from the night before, didn't let them pass.

Arms crossed over his chest, the brute, doused in a bottle of cologne, pungent enough to burn any and all nose hairs, stood in their way.

"You're not allowed in."

"Why not? You let us in last night."

"Not happening today."

"But look…" Luna pulled out an ID card and waved it in front of his nose. "I brought my driver's license."

"Still not happening. Boss's orders."

"Charlemagne banned us?"

It explained a lot, not that Luna accepted it.

"This is a free country. You can't keep me out."

Actually, they could, and they could call the cops. At least Jeoff thought they might have given the distant sirens.

"Come on." Jeoff tugged at Luna's hand. "We'll go somewhere else."

Face set in a scowl, and scuffing her cowgirl boots, which looked utterly adorable paired with her jean skirt and plaid blouse tied off under her breasts, Luna stomped back in the direction of his car. "I can't believe we're walking away. I mean, we totally could have strong-armed him. Or at least I could have and you could have slipped inside and checked out his staff and stuff for more plain dudes." Plain dudes being her new word for the scentless fellows.

"Strong-arming wouldn't have worked."

"And scuttling off with our tails tucked will?" was her sarcastic retort.

Her lack of faith pricked. "I can't believe you'd think they'd scare me off that easily." He made a chiding noise. "I'm not giving up. But I am going to employ something called subterfuge. Let Charlemagne and his crew think they've chased us off, but in reality…" He gave her a grin. "We double back and sneak in another way."

"I like the way your mind works."

Except his mind couldn't budge the men stationed at the front and back of the building and another pair to guard each end of the alley. Add in more on the outside of doors and exits.

"I don't think they're going to leave," Luna grumbled from where she slouched in the passenger seat of his car.

"Apparently, we spooked Charlemagne."

"We should have strung him up by his heels when we had a chance."

"Probably, but we didn't. And all this extra muscle doesn't mean he's guilty of anything. Could just be him beefing up security because of what we told him."

"You think he's suddenly concerned about the well-being of his patrons?" A sneer pulled her lips.

"No, but I'll bet he's concerned about his. I wonder where he's staying."

"You still don't have a home address for him?"

"Nothing. But he said he was new to the area. Could be he's renting or even staying at a hotel. A lot of them cater to business types."

"You can call around looking for a hotel to admit they have him staying with them. Me, I'm going to wait and see if there's an opportunity to get inside the club."

"You are not getting rid of me that easily. I know the hotel thing is a haystack. I agree with your plan that we wait and watch. Charlemagne will have to leave eventually, and when he does, we'll follow and then corner him." This time, they wouldn't be caught by surprise. So he settled in to watch, a stakeout, something he'd done hundreds of times, but totally different when done with Luna. For one, the confines of his car proved too tight. He couldn't escape her fragrance. It swirled around him in a heady mix.

Smells so good. And I know those lips taste even better. Go in for a quick one. She's right there. So close.

He needed air.

Stepping out of his car, Jeoff heard her say, "Where are you going? Doesn't matter. I'm coming with you."

Fuck yes, I want her to come with me. On my cock, yelling my name.

Desire for her pulsed with a life of its own. Need made him want to snare her close and…

"I've got an idea."

So did he. His involved saying screw it to the stakeout and finding a bed. She was right. This attraction between them needed resolving. He couldn't concentrate. "What are you doing?" he asked as she grabbed him by the jacket and jerked him toward the lip of a narrow alley.

"Follow me and you'll see."

No light shone between the buildings, yet she navigated the abandoned wooden pallets and debris with ease. Night vision was such a perk, but it also showed the starkness of the place. Not a single bed or patch of soft grass in sight.

"Hopefully this thing is up to code," Luna muttered, letting go of him to grab a rung and stick her foot on the first step.

"We can't go up there." The rancid scent of the alley did a lot to revive his mental state and point out issues with their current plan. "We should stick by the car so we can be ready to leave at a moment's notice in case we need to follow someone."

"Oh please. I doubt he's leaving anytime soon.

The club's just getting going. Chances are Charlemagne is in for a while. At least up here, we can have a good view of who's coming and going. Not to mention, we won't look as suspicious. I mean, come on, you don't think they're going to notice us sitting in the car?"

They wouldn't think anything of it if the windows fogged and the car rocked on its springs. "I guess we can go up and take a look." A part of him felt as if he should point out that it would be chilly at the top. If they were going to fool around, they'd be warmer in his car. And that rationality alone was why he didn't argue any further.

If he stayed in that car with her so close by, he wouldn't be able to stop what would inevitably happen. Then again, he might have reached the point of no return anyway.

Luna twitched her tail, and he followed. In this case, he followed her up a ladder, a wooden and metal one, bolted to the side of the building. It creaked and shuddered as they clambered up the narrow rungs.

He didn't bother averting his gaze from her pert derriere as it moved ahead of him, flexing in utmost perfection. He might have drooled a little at the thought of it wiggling the same way naked. It appeared, where Luna was concerned, his resistance was almost entirely gone. It would take only a slight shove to tip him over the edge. Instead, her shove brought him close to a chimney that radiated heat on the roof and, given it sat close to the edge, meant they could stay warm while they watched.

"Did you know this was here?" he asked, noting the milk crates parked upside down on the space between the parapet and the chimney.

"An educated guess. Most buildings have some

kind of heating system, and this time of the year, they're pumping warmth into their warehouses trying to keep merchandise at temperature."

"You know, in all my years of stakeouts, it never occurred to me to get an aerial view. We usually stick to a car. Easier to follow."

"You gotta think outside the box, wolfie. In this case, you're assuming there's something to follow. In case you didn't notice yet, the club has no cars parked anywhere. None. Nada. Zilch. So either Charlemagne walks everywhere or he has to call a cab. Which means we have a minute or so when the taxi arrives to get our asses back down to your wheels. We have time, and if we don't nab him tonight, we'll get him tomorrow."

"Already planning another date?" He couldn't help but tease her, knowing how she panicked at the thought of something a little more serious.

"If this is your idea of a date, then maybe I've been missing out." Her lips split into a wide grin. "You have to admit, this is a much better view of the action."

She won that argument. Being discreet meant they couldn't park right outside the club. They would have gotten pegged right away. But up here, hiding in the shadows? It was a great spot for spying—and for lovers.

Alone. At last.

Must resist.

Fuck that.

Jeoff tired of resisting. Tired of his own damned rules and morals. He hadn't felt himself since he started spending time with Luna. On the contrary, he felt frustrated and anxious and aroused and alive. So fucking alive.

It wasn't just felines who suffered from curiosity. He did too. He wanted to know what it would feel like if he just let go with her. If he said screw it and made love to her like he'd been fantasizing.

Here and now. Why wait?

Before logic could foil his need, he drew Luna to him, dragged her into his arms, and slanted his mouth over hers, finding her lips pliant and willing.

A part of him recognized what they did was dangerous, and not because they kissed in plain sight of the club that might be involved in the kidnapping and disappearance of folk. The embrace bordered on dangerous because he knew he couldn't stop and knew he would want more.

All of her. I want all of her. Say goodbye to the single life. It didn't matter if Luna thought they would only enjoy a fling, that this would be something they'd do a few times and then get bored of.

He knew better. *She's it for me.*

The realization, the one he kept denying, was why he'd fought for so long. Once he sank into her, took Luna and made her his, that was it. She would totally ruin him for other women. No question about it.

And he'd ruin any guy who thought he could have her—with his fist.

Priding himself on having a cool head only applied where Luna wasn't concerned. Touch her, and he would go rabid.

Chapter Thirteen

Luna had pretty much convinced herself she was done trying to seduce Jeoff. The man seemed content on torturing the two of them, determined to send her the most mixed signals ever, so when he cupped her face and drew her lips to his, she fully expected a torrid kiss followed by intense sexual frustration.

The understanding didn't mean she pushed him away. She couldn't. The touch of his mouth on hers ignited a fire within her, a wild primal urge to place her mark on this male, to make him her own.

There was a height difference between them that he solved by lifting her. Since she didn't want him to drop her, she wrapped her legs around his waist. That was her logic, but the reality was, not only did it bring her lips in line with his, it also pressed the core of her against him—against the hardest part of him.

No denying his arousal for her. What she did worry about was if this was going to be another exercise in frustration. It wasn't just men who had parts turning blue.

In between kisses, she managed to ask, "What are we doing?"

"What's it look like we're doing?" was his answer.

Not exactly the most revealing of answers. "It looks like we're kissing"—nibble and suck—"but the last time we got this close"—tug of his lower lip—

"you walked away." She might die if he did that to her again.

"I'm done fighting this. I'm not going anywhere, not this time. Not ever."

What was that supposed to mean?

Asking for an explanation would have to wait. He deepened the embrace, his mouth claiming hers with a fiery touch, a possessive hunger that she also felt. Kissing Jeoff was unlike anything she'd ever experienced, and she'd experienced a lot.

Why the difference? Why the sensation of sitting on a precipice of importance?

The intensity of the moment frightened. The implication that this would lead to something more terrified. Was she ready for this? Ready for Jeoff and everything he promised?

For all the teasing they'd done, she'd never actually imagined it would happen. Hoped it would, but never thought beyond the fantasy.

What happens after we have sex? Jeoff no longer resisted. On the contrary, he seduced, but he'd made it clear what his intentions were. He wanted a relationship. Question was, did she? Perhaps she could convince him to try something more casual? Would that be enough for him, or would he expect something more of her, something deeper?

What do I want of him?

Was forever too much?

A thing called doubt, not something she experienced very often, thought she should move away, put some space between them. Get a few breaths of air and clear her head.

Ha. No. No way was she moving away from the lips slanted over hers. How could she resist the teasing and nibbling, the sensual exploration of her mouth? The answer was she couldn't. Make that wouldn't. But he sensed her withdrawal, and he stopped the embrace long enough to say, "Are you all right? Do you want me to stop?"

"You'd stop?"

"I would if you asked."

Because he respected her. Hot damn.

"Don't you dare stop now." She'd never wanted a man this bad.

"Or else what?" he teased, his breath feathering across her lips.

She wound her arms around his neck and tugged him close, mashing her mouth to his. Jeoff groaned, a hum of appreciation that she absorbed with parted lips that allowed a sinuous foray by his tongue. The intimacy of the French kiss made her toes curl as the taste of him drove her wild. The tips of her fingers dug into his back as she clung to him. Annoying clothes separated their skin. The horror. The irritation.

She dragged her lips away and nibbled along the clean-shaven edge of his jaw. Somehow, he'd found the time today to run a razor over it. A shame, she wouldn't have minded the friction of his bristles. Her lips kept moving, and he tilted his head back, baring his throat in the ultimate gesture of trust.

She let her tongue flick over the rapid pulse beating in his neck. She pressed her lips to it, the predator in her pleased that he didn't try to bend her to his will. In that moment, he belonged to her.

We should mark him. Now.

His smooth column would look so good with a set of teeth marks. Hers.

The suggestion had her gasping and pulling back. She needed to put space between them before she did something she'd regret. However, he didn't know the evil thoughts that floated in her brain and didn't see the mental battle waging inside her head. He pursued her for another torrid kiss, melting her resistance. Resistance was foolish.

She wanted this. She'd just make sure she didn't bite him.

Should have brought a muzzle.

Holding her in mid-air meant she could grope him, but he couldn't let his hands rove her body. Perhaps that explained why he abruptly sank to the rooftop, folding his legs so that she sat in his lap, still straddling him.

She unfisted the fabric of his jacket so that her fingers were free to roam upward, sifting through the fine strands of his hair. He proved less subtle in his exploration, palming her ass cheeks and squeezing. He pulled her tight to his body, their position decadently intimate. Since her skirt rode up around her hips, that left only her tiny panties as a barrier to her sex, and the material was hopelessly soaked. He got to wear some of that moisture, as his jeans, the thick, impenetrable denim, absorbed some of it. Could he feel the heat that radiated from her?

He squeezed her ass, and she couldn't help but quip, "Those aren't oranges. No need to test them."

"Less testing and more like admiring. Do you have any idea how long I've wanted to grab your ass?"

A spurt of enjoyment heated her at his admission. "If you think those are nice, wait until I get you between my thighs and I squeeze." Too late, she wondered if she'd scare him off with her brazenness.

He let out a low chuckle against her lips. "I look forward to it."

A reply on her part turned into a gasp as he let his lips dart to the lobe of her ear. He nipped the tip and drew a moan of pleasure. He'd found her weak spot. And he totally exploited it.

As he tortured the shell of her ear, she pressed tighter to him, the buds of her nipples chafing at the fabric covering them. She burned with need. She so wanted him to touch them.

Leaning back, she untied her shirt, slipped the buttons free, and stripped it off, leaving her sitting in his lap in only her skirt, bra, and panties. Even without the hot chimney at his back, she would have stayed warm with the look in his eyes.

He devoured her with his gaze, the hot glance scorching her skin in awareness. He slid his hands up from her buttocks to her ribs, stopping at the edge of her bra. It wasn't the first time a man touched her, yet Luna couldn't help but tremble at his caress. His seeking hands slid around to her back. With deft fingers, he unhooked the bra and shed it, freeing her breasts.

She leaned back and licked her lips in invitation. A hint of a smile lurked around his lips, but his eyes were firmly on the prize. He cupped her breasts, a perfect handful for each of his palms. His thumb brushed over the peak of her nipple; the already tight bud pulled even tauter. At the pinch between fingers and the roll, she moaned. At the tug of her nipples, she felt a jolt between her thighs.

"You are so fucking gorgeous." He practically growled the words. He needn't have bothered. She could read the heated worship in his gaze, but he wanted to do more than look. He wished to pay homage with his mouth. As his head dipped forward, she arched her back to present her breasts to him. Jeoff took what she offered, his mouth latching onto a protruding nipple, sucking it with his warm, wet mouth. Her other taut bud did not languish as his fingers toyed with it, teasing her to pleasurable heights. She couldn't help her sounds of enjoyment, and he seemed to like her audible encouragement, as he grew bolder with his caresses.

When he buried his face in her cleavage, she hugged him close and wished he'd bury his face elsewhere. Mmm. Just the thought had her pushing free and standing.

"What are you—"

She muffled his question by digging her hand into his hair and pulling him to the vee of her thighs. He got the hint and hit his knees, a supplicant eager to worship. Her skirt remained pushed up around her waist, exposing her arousal-soaked panties. He hooked his fingers and yanked, pulling them down the length of her legs, but leaving them tethered around her ankles and boots. His fingers dug into her thighs, holding and spreading her, exposing her to his view. He nuzzled her, rubbing his face against her mound, teasing her with his warm breath. He managed to wedge his tongue between her thighs, the slick tip of it tagging her nether lips.

"Yes." She practically purred the word over and over as he lapped at her, the wet strokes of his tongue insistent. She quivered, all of her primed and ready for more.

More as in him, sinking into her. Now. No more delay.

She pushed him away, and he growled. "I'm not done."

"No, you're not." She managed to pivot without falling, her ankles still tethered by her panties. She bent over and braced her hands on the parapet, knowing she exposed her core. She heard him suck in a breath. A glance over her shoulder, a come-hither invitation, was all he needed to take what she offered.

He rose from the rooftop, hands on the closure for his pants. He unbuttoned and pushed at his pants until he sprang gloriously free, his thick cock bobbing in appreciation.

"What do you know? You were right. You don't pass out when it's hard."

"Are you seriously teasing me at a moment like this?" He stood behind her and slapped the head of his cock off her ass. "You do realize you're at my mercy."

"About time. So do you mind canning the talk and getting to the action?"

"No respect," he grumbled. He continued to tap his hard shaft off her ass cheeks, but he also felt between her thighs, the tips of his fingers sliding along her sex. Just when she thought she might yell if he didn't do something, he wrapped an arm around her waist and hoisted her higher. Only then did he nudge her wet slit with the tip of his cock. At the feel of his thickness, she couldn't help but shudder, and a quiver made her channel clench tight, making it harder for him to push in.

"It's not going to fit," she couldn't help but say with disbelief.

"It will fit." Such determined words.

He dropped back to his knees, and with her still bent over, he plied his tongue against her, giving her sex a quick lashing that had her moaning. When he turned his attention to only her clit, the thrust of his fingers inside her sex had her gasping, especially when he went from two, to three, to a channel-stretching four.

Moans erupted from her as he pumped her

sweet flesh. This time, when he abruptly stood and the tip of him pushed, she didn't tense, and he eased himself into her tight channel. And she meant tight.

Jeoff stretched her, stretched her so delightfully with his sizable cock. Her fingers held tight to the parapet as she shoved herself back against him. She could feel him holding back, probably because of some misguided belief he'd hurt her. He'd learn she could handle it a little rough. Actually, she liked it when a lover didn't take it too slow and gentle. How better to show him how she liked it than to rock hard back against him, deeply sheathing his cock.

While she couldn't see it, she heard it as Jeoff let out a howl, not the most discreet sound and so surprising. So deeply satisfying. She made him lose control. Good, because he did the same to her. As Jeoff kept burying himself, over and over, the thickness of him thrusting in a cadence that stuttered her breath, she could only bask in the impending ecstasy, knowing that the tight coiling in her, the stringing of every single nerve, would culminate in the most ridiculous orgasm ever. If he would finally let go.

"Take me," she growled. Thrust. "Fucking take, wolfie. Take me hard and fast. Fuck me and make me your bitch. I want you to make me scream." The filthy words came out of her, but she couldn't stop them. The question was, would they frighten him away?

Like hell. Jeoff let out another howl of pleasure. His fingers clutched her and kept her perfectly poised for the rapid pumping of his hips. He slammed into her, a constant friction that had her keening. For once, a man gave Luna what she damned well wanted. He pounded at her flesh, hitting that sweet spot with each deep stroke. His body slapped against her ass with a smacking of flesh.

She rocked with him, her body so in tune with his that even her spirit, the very essence of her, seemed to have stretched to wrap around Jeoff, feeding her his emotions. She could feel his response to her sighs and moans, his intense pleasure at being with her.

It made her climax, made her squeeze his already tightly sheathed cock even closer. Having him buried to the hilt as she came meant something perfect to quiver around. Something to grip. It made her tumble over the edge of bliss, again and again, the first orgasm rolling over and over with each clench around him, and when he pulsed, the heat of his essence filling her, she shattered.

She might have collapsed if he hadn't wrapped himself around her shuddering body. He held her close to him, letting her recover as she strove to calm her harsh breaths. It was a strangely intimate moment.

And he ruined it by talking.

Chapter Fourteen

"Are you okay?" It seemed like a reasonable question seeing as how he'd completely lost control. How could he have done that to her, pound at her sweet flesh—pummeling her sex with his cock, unable to resist that wet haven—and without any regard for her? Never mind she'd asked him to go hard. A gentleman should, at the very least, inquire if his lover had come through the experience unscathed.

But this was Luna, and she didn't appreciate his courtesy. "Am I okay? Are you for real?" Luna righted herself. "Of course I'm all right. I'm not a delicate fucking flower, you know." She blasted him with words, and something struck him in that moment.

How often did Luna throw out shocking accusations or solicitations? Could that brazenness be part of protecting herself? Here she was faced with a moment of intimacy, and she didn't know how to react. She feared allowing herself to enjoy it. But why? Why would she do that? "I don't know why you're pissed. I was just showing you some basic politeness."

"Like you'd show anyone." Luna's shoulders drooped in uncharacteristic defeat. "You're probably this nice with everyone you screw. It means nothing." It was almost as if she spoke to herself.

"What the hell are you talking about now? I'm not being nice to you because I have to. I'm being courteous with you because I fucking care. Do you get that, Luna? I. Fucking. Care." He did, more than he could have imagined.

"If you care so much, then why have you been pushing me away?"

He scrubbed a hand through his hair. "Why? I told you why. Because I knew having sex with you would make things complicated."

"How? I'm not asking for anything from you."

"You're not, and yet you make me want more. And that's scary for me. Being with you is like inviting a hurricane into my life."

She planted her hands on her hips and should have looked ridiculous with her hair straggling in stray blonde wispy curls. She stood topless, her chest heaving, her nipples tight buds he longed to suck, and her skirt still up around her waist, baring her neatly trimmed mound. "So I'm a destructive force of nature? Gee, shower me with compliments, why don't you?"

"I would, but you'd probably emasculate me if I did."

"You're right, I would. I don't need you telling me how great I am. I know I'm awesome." Her chin tilted stubbornly.

"Yes, you are." He agreed, and yet she roasted him with a fiery glare.

"Awesome, and yet not good enough for Mr. Prissy Pants."

"Oh, kitten, you are more than perfect enough for me." He uttered the nickname he knew she hated, but couldn't resist, not when she looked so spitting-mad cute. He drew her toward him, but she was having none of that.

"Oh no you don't. No cuddling allowed. Don't think I don't see what you're trying to do."

"Trying to get lucky a second time?"

She shook her head. "Not happening. I told you we only needed to do it once to scratch our itch. I, for one, feel perfectly satiated." She indulged in the world's fakest stretch. "I am completely satisfied now that we've gotten it out of the way. With the sexual tension gone, we will be able to focus on our job."

"You do realize you standing there half naked isn't quite convincing me of that."

He reached out and attempted to flick a nipple. She danced out of reach, hands tugging at her ruched-up skirt.

"I don't think we should do that."

"Wow, that sounds like something I used to say." He couldn't help the mocking grin.

The scowl she presented made his smile only wider. "I think you were right. We should maintain our distance."

"What's this? Rejecting me after you took advantage of my poor, defenseless body?"

The snort she uttered held disbelief. "Whoa, wait a second. What defenseless body? There is nothing about you that needs protecting."

"What about my heart?"

"Don't mistake it for your ego. I think you're just crushed that I was right. One quick bump and grind and, presto, I am cured of you."

She might claim she didn't crave him anymore, yet he didn't believe it. He crossed his arms over his chest. "You're lying."

"Am not."

"Are too."

"Well, you can't prove it." She tossed her head with a stubbornness he'd come to expect—and enjoy.

"I think I can. If you're not into me anymore,

then come over here and kiss me."

"There will be no kissing. Don't embarrass yourself by begging."

"I don't beg."

"Then this conversation is over." Luna grabbed her shirt from the rooftop and threaded her arms through it. "Time to get back to work."

"Fuck work." Dealing with this brushoff suddenly seemed a hell of a lot more important.

"We've already fucked around long enough. Look, I think the club is starting to slow down. There's a bunch of cars leaving and—"

"I don't give a fuck. I want to deal with this. You and me. Right now."

"There is no you and me." She began to walk away from him to where the railing of the ladder curved over the parapet.

"Oh no you don't." It took only a couple of long strides to bring him within reach. He snared her arm and spun her to face him. "Why are you determined to avoid talking about us continuing what we started and having a relationship? You were the one who kept pushing until I caved. Now that I have, you're pushing me away."

"A relationship?" Her nose wrinkled. "Can't a girl just scratch an itch?"

There she went being deliberately crude, trying to distance herself from him. But he wouldn't let her. "Fine. We won't call it a relationship. How about we exclusively booty call for a while? Think of it as saving time. I have needs. You have needs. Why not take care of those needs together?" He used her own logic against her.

"That won't work."

"Why not?" Pathetic, yes, yet he couldn't stop

himself from asking. A part of him knew he should walk away. *I should leave her alone.* Let her deny what they could have. But if he walked, would he lose the chance to see if the two of them could become something great? What if Luna was it? What if he never found another woman who brought him alive? Who made him want—her, a future, a family, a forever—so fiercely?

Under stubborn in the dictionary, you'd find Luna. She drew herself tall. "Because. And before you keep pestering, has it occurred to you that perhaps I'm not interested because the sex sucked? Maybe I'm trying to dump you nicely."

A lesser man might have slunk away, crushed by the very thought. Jeoff knew better. A teasing grin pulled his lips. "That lie was so huge I'm surprised your nose didn't grow. You loved what happened between us. Don't forget, I felt how hard you came on my cock."

Judging by the indrawn breath and the sudden pattering of her heart, she did too. "Okay, so maybe the sex was good—"

He arched a brow.

"Fine, it was great, but I'm still dumping you. This is too intense for me. I don't need or want a clingy man messing up my life."

"Clingy?" He snorted. "Now you're really grasping at straws. I think you're scared that you're going to like me and want to stay with me. I promise that's not as frightening as it sounds. If it helps, I do know how to cook and clean."

"Don't bribe me. That's not fair."

"Tempting me until you drove me out of my mind"—and pants—"wasn't fair either."

"Well, I'm done doing that. It's best we not

take things further. You work closely with the pride, and when it doesn't work out, you'll find it awkward."

The pessimism bothered him. "Why do you assume it wouldn't work?"

"Why do you assume it would?"

Because you're mine. A belief she didn't share.

She began to walk away from him, again. She gave up. The lioness, who usually fought to the last breath, gave up without even trying. *She's taking the coward's way out.* And he called her on it.

A clucking noise filled the silent void between them.

Hands held out in attack mode, she whirled and asked, "What was that sound?"

He clucked again and flapped his arms.

Amber eyes narrowed. "Are you calling me a chicken?"

Cluck. "If the chicken fits." *Cluck.* "You had no problem calling me out, so now I'm returning the favor. You are a coward when it comes to the concept of having a committed relationship." He didn't sugarcoat it. Luna would see through it in a second. She was a woman who liked the truth, unvarnished and real.

"Why are you being so stubborn about this?"

"Maybe I've been hanging around a certain lioness too long and I like it." Liked having her around more than his sanity, apparently. *A serene and stable mental state is overrated. Chaos is what truly makes life worth living.*

"What the hell am I going to do about you?"

"Do me," was what he planned to say, but the sudden snarl of warning by his inner wolf alerted him to danger. He shouted, "Watch out!"

From the dark sky, something dipped, a

whoosh of displaced air the only warning before clawed hands extended, reaching for Luna. Her quick reflexes came in handy.

At the shouted warning, she ducked and dove to the side. Just in time too! The creature clutched at empty air and pulled up, large wings flapping to hold it aloft.

"What the fuck is that?" Luna snapped. She stood in a half-crouch, knees bent and hands held up, fists primed and ready to defend.

"Damned if I know." In the feeble light, while distinct details were difficult to discern, he did get a general shape, but a shape that made no sense. What he saw appeared as a hybrid between a bat and a human. Almost as if the creature had achieved a very controlled half-shift. Impossible. Shifters were either beast or man. There was no in between. Sure, they could occasionally pop a claw or the teeth would stretch, maybe a guy would suddenly sprout a beard, but those were small, fleeting changes, usually brought on by strong emotion. Those kinds of sporadic tiny shifts were nothing compared to the bat dude. Half-bat, half-man.

It should have been impossible. Yet, the mocking evidence fluttered to the roof deck, massive leathery wings retracting to a spot behind its back, the tips jutting tall. Even without the soaring reminder, two giant feet clad in shit-kicking boots on the ground, the thing bore a menacing demeanor with wide shoulders, a thick physique, and evident musculature.

A bat dude on 'roids. Nice.

He locked gazes with the thing. In almost every culture, man or beast, there existed a certain tradition. Jeoff likened it to the, "Who's the man?" syndrome.

Staring, though, meant truly examining the face

before him, a face that proved mostly human, yet, at the same time, achieved a chilling alien aspect. Gray skin, the shade of wet slate, the surface riddled with whorls and lines, a motif that reminded Jeoff of an intricate thumbprint. Fascinating, as he wondered if it was natural or created designs. The eyes appeared freakish. The crimson slit of the pupil shone with baleful fire, the red glow a beacon in the night. Dark hair, cut short, showcased ears pointed at the tips. But this was no elf.

If Jeoff were to make any comparison, he'd say demon, and everyone knew what team the demons played for.

The moment of shock at the creature's appearance passed, and it didn't seem inclined to run away at the sight of Jeoff. A fight? So be it. Jeoff sprang into motion. He slid his hand inside his jacket, gripping the revolver that still sat in its holster, not having been removed during that frantic moment of lovemaking. He drew it and, with a practice earned in the range, aimed and fired.

Bang. The report, echoing loudly, proved a waste, as his bullet went wide of its mark. Jeoff would note it wasn't his aim that had been off, but rather the unexpected fact that the bat dude moved faster than the eye could follow. One second there in front of him, and the next almost a dozen feet to his left.

Before he could blink and adjust his stance, another blur.

Luna cried out. "Don't you even think of touching me, buddy." A warning most beings valuing their life smartly heeded.

Not their assailant.

Bat dude seemed determined to go for Luna. He lunged, once again the motions blurring fast, but

Luna managed to sidestep. Avoiding, though, didn't mean she ran away. She had too much stubborn courage for that.

The side effect of her sticking around meant her proximity prevented him from shooting. Jeoff's aim was good, but he couldn't take a chance he'd hit her. He sprinted toward the action, hoping for a better shot.

With a screamed, "I hate rats, especially ones with wings," Luna lunged at bat dude, probably intent on doing some martial arts thing. Luna was a capable woman, one not to be messed with—unless you were a giant bat dude with super speed.

The same surprise Jeoff felt was reflected in Luna's face when the bat thing ended up behind her with an arm wrapped around her throat. Her fingers scrabbled at the arm choking her, and her feet flailed. She did her best to slam her cowboy boots down on the guy's instep, but her shorter legs put her at a disadvantage. The setback led to her attempting a donkey kick, which, if it landed, would have cracked a knee. It missed because the bat dude was big enough to dangle her out of reach.

"Stop." The one-command word matched a flex in the bat dude's arm over Luna's throat.

Jeoff halted his mad rush and took measure of the situation, which meant looking at the guy and being struck anew by how human the dude seemed in spite of his leathery, dark skin and the massive tips of his wings jutting from his back.

"Let her go," he ordered. It never hurt to try and reason.

"I'm keeping the girl. Drop the gun or she dies." While gravelly, the words were perfectly spoken. No guttural or animalistic intonations.

"And how do I know you won't kill her anyhow?"

Wicked sharp teeth appeared in a smile made for nightmares. "You don't. And I probably will." The arm flexed, and he could see Luna's eyes bulge. "But only after I play with her first." The bat dude darted fast as a snake, his mouth opening wide and his long fangs sinking into the flesh of her shoulder exposed by the open neck of her shirt. The thing sucked at her, uttering little grunts. It was utterly insane, and so unexpected that Jeoff froze. He hesitated instead of acting out of fear the monster would go ballistic and tear out her throat.

But perhaps the slurping wasn't any better. He noted how Luna initially went stiff then softened, her eyelashes fluttering, in a sense acquiescing to the assault.

That more than anything snapped him out of his stupor because he knew Luna would never willingly allow this to happen. Jeoff yelled as he darted forward, only to watch in frustration as the bat dude launched himself into the air, a limp Luna clutched to its chest. He took aim and fired, aiming for the wings, wings that flapped, meaning the bullet missed.

Mocking laughter from the creature fueled his rage, but it was seeing the bat dude fly off, a limp Luna in tow, that saw Jeoff let loose a howl that echoed. He yelled a bestial cry of rage at his impotence. Wearing four feet or two, it didn't matter, he couldn't chase the winged enemy down. With his enemy taking the air, he didn't even have a trail to follow.

That beast is getting away with my woman.

The realization galled. How could he keep her safe if he had no way of knowing where the monster took Luna? But he'd wager he knew who had.

Someone at the club was involved. He stared over the parapet, noting a line of taxis out front as patrons took their leave, some of them too tipsy to drive. He also noted Charlemagne standing out front, acting nonchalant. He didn't buy it for a minute. Charlemagne might not have been the one who kidnapped Luna, but he knew something.

Hunt him down. Grab him by the neck and shake him until he talks.

It seemed like such a bold and wonderful plan, but it would also probably assure Luna's demise. That kind of primal mentality wouldn't help Luna.

Can it, furball. He sent a mental poke at his wolf because he could feel his raging beast pushing at the boundaries that kept him caged. Usually well behaved, his wolf was practically frothing, out of its mind and trying to take control of their body.

He understood its frustration. Luna was gone, and he had to find her, but to do so, he needed a location. Jeoff peeked down at the club. The club that seemed to be involved in everything.

My gut says Charlemagne is aware of what is going on, and he is going to damned well spill it. But he might need some help, especially since the man stepped back inside, surrounding himself with walls and probably a security force.

Despite the snarling prod of his wolf that demanded they go after Charlemagne, he did the right thing and put in a call to Arik first.

"What happened?" was the first thing Arik asked.

Both Jeoff and his wolf hung their heads in shame as they admitted their failure. Tonight, there was no roar from the pride leader, just a cold, quiet promise. "Tonight, we hunt."

The lions would not sleep tonight, not until Luna and her captor were found.

Showing patience after the phone call didn't come easy. The usually meticulous Jeoff wanted to rush into that club and start shaking people for answers. His rational self kept reminding he was outnumbered.

Those guarding the corners and the main door of the club saw him. It wasn't as if he hid himself. Jeoff planted himself right across from the club, leaning against the shuttered warehouse and staring at the door. He kind of hoped Charlemagne would emerge. While lots of humans did, most of them protesting the early curtailing of their evening activities, of the man he sought, not a sign. Some of those evicted chose to linger, the stream of smoke from their cigarettes hazing the air and masking scent. Did Luna's kidnapper walk amongst them? Was he already too late?

Why do we wait? A wolf might show the patience to stalk, but in this instance, it pushed at him to do something. Anything.

He couldn't act rash—even if he longed to cast off the chains of civility. He could only wait for reinforcements—the more, the merrier—to improve Luna's odds.

Lucky for him, Luna had lots of friends. The cavalcade of cars pulled up, a serious-looking brigade of high-end vehicles that spilled a mostly golden army. Varying in height and size, the tawny legion took over the sidewalk with the occasional dark and red hair adding a spot of color.

As Arik, with a toss of his golden mane, stepped from a pimped-out black SUV, Jeoff pushed off from his spot against the wall. The pride's vain leader had been growing out his locks since the mishap with the hairdresser—who was now his wife. Rumor had it she was carrying the next heir, but then again, the lionesses were convinced everyone who packed on a few pounds was pregnant.

Joining Arik were Hayder and Leo, the pride's beta and omega, here to provide support for one of their own. The other vehicles spilled mostly lionesses, the pride's true hunters and a fierce force when riled. Jeoff recognized more than a few like the cocoa-skinned Reba and the red-haired Stacey. He could almost guarantee they came because they wanted to. No need to order this crew to do their job. Lions were fiercely loyal, especially in this pride, the bonds that held them together under Arik's rule the strongest, or so Jeoff had heard.

Yet, it wasn't just friendship and loyalty drawing them to help. A hint of violence tinged the air, the one sure lure to bring the ladies. They did so love a good bar fight.

As the ladies of the pride commandeered the sidewalk, those straggling outside the building, having a cigarette and waiting for a cab, scattered. Smart people. No one wanted to get in the way of a golden wave.

Jeoff crossed the street to greet Arik and his entourage.

"Have you seen anything?" Arik asked with a glance at the club.

"Nothing."

"Are we sure Charlemagne is in there?"

"No." Jeoff could watch only one door at a time.

"But you're convinced he knows what took Luna?"

"Yes." Call it gut instinct or desperate hope. Charlemagne was the only thing Jeoff had that might give him a clue as to Luna's whereabouts.

"Good enough for me." Arik strode toward the door, only to have the two bouncers manning it close in to form a barrier before it.

The bigger of the two blocked his path. "We are not taking any more guests for the night."

A golden brow tilted. "Are you denying me passage?"

Arms crossed over chests seemed to be the reply.

Jeoff almost laughed because he knew what would happen next. Arik twitched his fingers, and with a slinky grace only felines could achieve, the lionesses strutted forth.

"Since I don't lower myself to taking care of minions…" Arik sniffed. "Ladies, would you mind?"

Before the guys blocking the way could react, a lioness contingent swarmed them. Poor bastards.

Jeoff and Arik spent a moment watching the fight.

"They are faster than humans. Shifter fast," Arik observed as one of the fellows managed to clip Reba—it only served to enrage her.

"And scentless."

"Strange. I wonder if that is part of their camouflage system," Arik mused aloud.

"Doesn't explain the biting." Jeoff couldn't get it out of his mind.

"Maybe they're vampires." Hayder interjected. "They like to suck necks, don't they?"

They all winced as Stacey wound up a knee and sank it into the smaller bouncer's nut sac.

"Vampires don't exist," Leo muttered.

"Neither do bat dudes," Jeoff retorted.

Reba clocked the big guy in the face, and as he staggered back, Joan stuck her foot out and tripped him. Moments later, the doorway into the club was clear.

"Shall we?" As leader of the pride, Arik wasn't allowed to lead the way in, not because they feared for his safety, because they all knew Arik could take care of his own skin. But by sending his soldiers ahead, he sent a message—*I am important*. As Arik had once explained to Jeoff, sometimes it wasn't about actual strength, but the impression of it that proved most important.

With the path clear, the lionesses pushed and shoved to get through the door first, determined to tackle any danger waiting. Clear disappointment shone on their faces as they penetrated the first ring and encountered nothing.

The outer vestibule vibrated as the club still rocked the tunes, catchy with a lively bass. The pulsing beat had no effect on him this time. As if he would dance while Luna was in danger.

The pride flowed through the next set of doors and bypassed the coat check area right into the club proper. They spread out across the dance floor, commandeering the space and surrounding the few remaining humans. A few too many witnesses for what might happen. The humans had to go, and in a way that didn't leave a mark.

To help in that process, Stacey took over the DJ booth. The music came to a sudden stop. In the void left behind, people asked, "What happened? Where's the music?"

Microphone in hand, Stacey waved from behind the booth's window as she spoke huskily to the crowd. "Sorry, folks. Department of Health here for a random inspection. We ask that you kindly grab your coats and leave in an orderly fashion."

It might have worked if some smartass hadn't yelled, "It's a raid!"

The horde of lions watched with no little disdain as the humans rampaged for exits. Apparently, more than a few were concerned about getting nabbed in the raid. As for Jeoff, he would never understand the allure of mind-altering drugs.

You drink beer.

Totally different thing. And, yeah, he was okay with being a hypocrite.

The antics of the fleeing humans did not concern him. He did note that a few non-pride shifters already in the club, while keeping to the outskirts, remained behind. Apparently, they thought they should bear witness to what happened next.

What happened next was the club emptied, leaving only those who could swap into fur behind. Not even a single employee could be seen or smelled. Jeoff didn't like it. Where had everyone gone? Surely they hadn't fled like yellow-bellied cowards?

Arik planted his hands on his hips and bellowed, "Gaston Charlemagne, you are summoned by the king of this city. Show yourself." As pompous announcements went, Arik got just the right note of arrogance.

But no reply was forthcoming.

"Are you sure he's still here?" Arik asked, frowning.

"Yes." Jeoff's gut insisted. "But apparently, he's got this thing about dealing with what he terms animals."

"Who's an animal?" Leo asked.

"Apparently, you in bed. Your woman isn't shy about sharing details." Hayder made a clicking sound and added a wink-wink, nudge-nudge motion.

Despite Meena's open ways, Leo still managed a heightened color of embarrassment. "Don't believe a word she says."

"Who cares if Leo's the man in the bedroom? We should spread out and find Charlemagne," Reba snapped.

"How are we supposed to find him if he doesn't stink?" Hayder queried.

"Tear the place apart. If he's in here, we'll find him."

Apparently, the threat of destruction was enough to draw attention. "Do you mind not sending your feline goons to destroy my place of business? As it is, your antics have cost me revenue for my coffers this evening." At the words spoken amidst them, more than one lion fanged, their inner beast pushing for dominance and baring teeth. Arik and his inner circle were the only ones to remain unaffected—or faking it super well. Cats were known masters at the art of nonchalance.

Jeoff didn't react much, given he had half expected a dramatic entrance. Still, though, how the fuck did the guy just waltz into the middle of them with no one noticing? And where did he get the balls to do that? Only the suicidal would put themselves amidst some riled lions.

"You are Charlemagne, I take it." Arik perused him head to toe. "Nice suit."

Indeed, gone was the casual wear of the morning. Charlemagne now wore a fitted suit, which gave him a certain elegance that put them all to shame.

"I don't think you came to discuss the perfect

form of my garments. State your business and leave."
The slightly accented words were spoken with utmost
confidence.

Perhaps that worked with other people, but
now he was dealing with lions. Arrogance was Arik's
middle name. The lion king prowled around
Charlemagne, who, to his credit, didn't stiffen or turn,
even when the predator paced behind him.

Returning to a spot in the front, Arik stopped.
"Jeoff tells me you know of our kind."

"Yes, I know all about your animal kingdom
and don't particularly care. The affairs of animals do
not concern me."

"And perhaps that was an acceptable attitude
wherever you emigrated from, but here"—Arik smiled,
the cold grin of a predator—"we have rules. My
rules."

"What do I care of your rules?"

"You should care because this city is mine. I
own it, and that means you have to obey. And one of
the rules says if you're not human, then you report to
me."

"What makes you think I'm not human?"

More than one snort of disbelief echoed, Arik's
loudest of all. "Let's not play this game. I know you're
not human."

"Perhaps not, and yet I can assure you that I
don't share my mind with some primal creature."

"Are you trying to claim you're not related to
that bat dude?" Jeoff pressed.

"Bat dude?" Rich laughter flowed from
Charlemagne, velvety smooth and tickling the senses.
More than one person shifted at the sound. "I rather
like that and might use it. And, to answer your
question, I am not a whampyr."

"A wham what?" Hayder asked.

"Whampyr. That is what you call servants with certain abilities."

"Servants for who?"

The smug grin on Charlemagne's face could have rivaled Arik's.

All it did was annoy Jeoff. "They serve him, obviously. But the more important thing is if he knows what they are then that means he knows who took Luna."

"A whampyr took the female I met this morning?" Charlemagne's expression switched from mocking to serious. "When? Where?"

"Almost right across the street from the rooftop we were staked out on."

"Abducted in plain sight? Unacceptable." Charlemagne whirled and snapped his fingers. A big brute drifted down from the ceiling, large stone gray wings slowing his descent. It seemed Jeoff wasn't the only one who'd missed him perched overhead. A bunch of the lionesses crouched and rumbled with discontent.

"Milord has orders?" the big dude asked.

"Head count. Now. I want to know who is missing."

Low, menacing growls and hisses filled the room with impending menace as bodies clad in black wear with the club logo on their breasts emerged from pockets of shadow. Scentless and quiet, a perfect dozen in total, with Charlemagne as the thirteenth.

Of the twelve, only three bore a bat shape— the captain of the whams and two more, none of whom were the right size or look for the bat dude Jeoff had seen on the roof.

"Is one of your staff missing?" Arik asked

Charlemagne as Jeoff perused the expressions on the human faces. Could they all turn into giant bats? And were they truly not shifters as Charlemagne claimed?

"All of my servants are accounted for. Perhaps your pet dog is mistaken."

"I know what I saw." Jeoff pushed forward. "Unless there are more bat dudes than these running around the city, then someone here did it."

"If what you claim is true, then one of my servants is committing the most foul insubordination." Charlemagne fixed his gaze on his people.

"It is not insubordination to want to feed." The unassuming fellow suddenly snapped his head up from his subservient pose, and his eyes blazed. The resemblance was faint, his human guise somehow narrower of face and more aquiline of nose, but there was no mistaking the expression or the words.

The club owner's face turned cold and hard. "We do not feed from the animals."

"Too late. We have already had a taste." The guy licked his lips. "They were delicious. And you, the master who thinks he knows everything, never had a clue. We stole the animals from under your nose, from this very club."

At the admission, many of the lionesses growled and pressed forward. Arik held up his hand, and they halted, but their gazes promised retribution. "You're the one who emptied their houses and wiped them clean?" Arik asked.

A sneer curled the lips of the male confessing. "My friends and I have learned a few things about covering our tracks. This isn't the first city we've played in, but those were the first of your kind. And not the last."

It was all Jeoff could do to not dive at the guy

and tear out his throat. Only knowing his death would assure Luna's stayed his paw.

Patience, my wolf.

It seemed Charlemagne was less than impressed by the knowledge his servants had acted without permission. "Treason against your master is punishable by death."

"What we have done is not treason, but a change in command. We tire of your rules. It is time we commanded the weak on Earth, as we were meant to."

"We? Who is this we?" Charlemagne sneered. "I see the blood you ingested has addled your wits because you seem to forget I made you. I can unmake you."

"Not if we kill you first. Kill him!" screamed the fucker.

And that was when all hell broke loose. Mostly because the lionesses recognized a challenge when they heard one. Black fabric went flying as bodies morphed into giant bats. It seemed like most of Charlemagne's servants were part of this rebellion. They hissed, fangs long and menacing before lunging for Charlemagne, who, in a single blink of an eye, just wasn't there. But the attacking whams did find someone willing to fight.

Lionesses dove on the winged bats, most having traded soft skin for softer fur. Those intent on rebellion fought with grim intensity, their incredible strength and speed making the lionesses truly employ their finest skills. A duo of the whams appeared to have surrounded Charlemagne, who frowned but did nothing to stop the carnage of his treasonous servants. The outcome seemed certain, the golden army outnumbering the whams, which was perhaps why one of them, Jeoff noted, was trying to get away. The one Jeoff needed alive.

He ran after the leader of the rebellion, his voice a guttural growl. "Where is Luna? Where did you put her?"

"Nowhere you can reach, dog," was the mocking reply.

As the bat dude whirled, looking for an exit that didn't require him dying, Jeoff got close enough to lunge. The fucker was too fast. The beast took wing, soaring to a spot too high for Jeoff's leap to reach. For the second time that day, he had to watch as the monster bested him.

He's getting away.

And there was nothing he could do about it. High above, the monster smashed one of the blacked-out windows, escaping into the night sky. Despite how fast Jeoff ran for the outside, he couldn't see where the bat dude went. And he was no closer to finding Luna.

Fuck.

Chapter Fifteen

That fucking hurts. The side of Luna's head throbbed, a painful and ignoble reminder of her defeat. It was enough to make her want to go back to sleep.

Wake up. Her inner lioness slapped at her.

She wrinkled her nose. *Don't do that. Wanna sleep.* The lethargy in her body was much too compelling to ignore.

Rouse yourself. We're in danger. An insistent cry by her lioness that Luna only sluggishly responded to. She just couldn't seem to make herself care. There might not be sunshine drugging her into taking a nap, but there was definitely something urging her to keep her eyes shut and relax.

We can't relax. He's going to come back.

He who? Jeoff? She wouldn't mind him coming to snuggle with her. She might even share her sunny spot with him. Especially if it got him naked.

Jeoff naked was so much fun to look at. Even better to touch.

Seriously? Her feline seemed less than impressed with her fond thoughts of Jeoff. It kept yowling about danger.

Tell you what. Why don't you take care of it? While she floated on lazy waves.

Ugh. Such disgust from her lioness, but, at the same time, relief. Apparently, if Luna wasn't in the mood to drive, then her cat was. Without further ado, her beast side thrust herself past the feeble human shell until limbs burst free of the silly clothing that bound it and paws slipped out of confining boots.

Shaking a tawny head, the lioness stood on her four feet and peeked around. The painful act of change apparently provided the right kind of slap because she noted that, within her mind, her fleshy self struggled to remove the sluggish chains binding her and pay more attention.

Hold on a second. Where are we?

In a very bad place. The lioness couldn't help but snort. The bad called to her curiosity. What had passed through here?

Nose to the floor, she checked out the space, noting the room was large enough to walk around, but not by much. The only light came from a hole in the wall that allowed scant illumination. Since it was closest, she checked it first and recoiled as she noted the edge of the opening sheared off. Peeking down, she uttered an irritated snarl. Too high to jump and, since she didn't know how many lives she had left, probably not her best option.

Whirling, she allowed her eyes to adjust for the darkness.

Wood-covered openings in the walls—*those are windows*, her other self yammered—preventing escape. An open door led to a tiled room, not very large with a large dry basin and another hard shell holding only the molded residue of water.

It didn't smell good at all. And there was no exit in here, just like there was no exit in the next room beside it. So far, a bunch of little chambers that taunted and exhilarated because she'd been challenged. This place thought to defeat her. But conceding was never a choice. There had to be another exit. The fleshy habitats, even abandoned ones, always had an entrance. Returning to the first room, the one with a still gaping hole in the wall, still too high to jump, she stopped and let her head rotate side to side, her eyes filtering the ambient light and shadows to see.

The food preparation area showed no exit. The storage cabinets were exposed, the doors to them hanging lopsidedly or completely torn off.

Taking a step to the far side of the room, she winced at a loud creak. She halted, distributing her weight to all four paws and feeling her position. No further cracking, but she lowered her nose and sniffed. Rot. So much rot.

Watch the walking. The floor proved precarious, parts of it rotted, the boards sinking under her weight. Having already explored behind her, she logically noted that there was now only one opening left to explore. One more chance to find a path to escape that didn't involve trying to climb down a smooth surface from a great height.

As with all the other openings, the barrier to it—*door, remember we had those lessons? It's a door*—leaned against the wall across from it. Sticking her nose out showed only more decay and more openings to explore. Above, the ceiling had partially collapsed, debris and the itchy pink stuff blocking one direction. Looking the other way, she noted a dark opening from which wafted a rank stench that almost colored the air with its foul miasma.

Ooh what's that? While she wouldn't mind going for a peek, the voice of the squishy one advised caution.

The lioness might have ignored it if not for the teensiest of sounds right behind her.

Who dares to come so close?

Preservation controlling her motions, she whirled and dashed at the bulky dark figure standing there, only to miss tearing out his heart as he leaped nimbly out of reach.

Come back. She wasn't done playing.

Neither was he apparently. The thing with no scent reached out and tweaked the tip of her tail, a hard-yanked challenge.

He dares touch my tail! The squishy one inside her was absolutely enraged.

A low snarl rumbled past peeled lips as she pivoted and narrowed her amber gaze on the *thing* that had dared bring her here. The *thing* that dared mess with a lioness. *Rowr!*

Keeping her gaze locked on the *thing*, she darted toward him again, but never made it all the way, as part of the floor splintered and her paw went ramming through the rotted fibers. A startled yelp escaped her, the pain sharp as her forward momentum was rudely halted. To add insult to injury, she was stuck. She yanked at her trapped paw, only to hiss in pain as the wooden splinters dug into her skin.

The squishy one soothed her ruffled fur. *Let me help you.*

"Is the kitty cat caught?" The human-shaped mouse with wings—*because I refuse to call him a bat!*—walked toward her. There was something incongruous about a monster wearing black stone-washed jeans and running shoes but no shirt. The normal gear seemed only to emphasize the strangeness of his appearance.

Says the woman who can change into a lioness.

Speaking of lion, better get that paw unstuck so she wouldn't be at a complete disadvantage. The form swap happened quickly, and even better, she survived it. She'd hoped he wouldn't use that in-between time inherent in every morph to kill her.

Good news, her hand slid free of the hole, albeit sporting a few embedded wooden pieces. All her limbs free, though, didn't mean she changed back into her beast. If she couldn't dominate as an animal, then perhaps she could outthink her foe. And another cool thing she could do better in her human shape? Glare, which was what she did from under a hank of hair

Never look afraid. A rule to live by.

"Who are you? How did I get here?" Like, seriously, how had she gotten here? Last Luna recalled, the flying mouse had her in a chokehold and then tried to give her a hickey. The reminder had her slapping a hand over her neck. The jagged edges from a pair of punctures rose from her skin, dry and healing, but the skin still noticeably swollen. "You bit me!"

"I intend to do more than that, kitty cat. I always wondered why the master said your kind was off-limits. I assumed it was because you were less than tasty. But now I know the truth." The gray-faced guy cupped his denim-clad groin and leered at her. "You taste delicious. Especially when fresh." He licked his lips, and Luna knew the proper response for a normal person was to shudder, maybe even cringe.

Normal. Such an overrated word.

Luna gave him the finger. "Up yours. No one is taking any bites out of this body." Unless his name was Jeoff. For him, she'd make an exception, if he'd still have her. She seemed to recall dumping him before her inadvertent capture.

I might have been hasty. Perhaps we should pursue this a little further. Or at least have more awesome sex.

Of course, sex would happen only if she lived past the next few minutes.

"Your feisty nature is so compelling. The other

couples I snared with my comrades didn't have the same fire as you and that dog."

Nice to know attitude flavored the flesh. And to think, all this time, people thought it was garlic that kept them away. "If we're so yummy-looking, then why did you chicken out and only grab me? Lack of balls? Couldn't handle us both?"

"I am not a coward. I chose to not take the wolf as a matter of taste. While his kind proved nice to eat, slightly nicer than humans, they definitely didn't have the same flavor as cat. Turns out I like pussy." He wanted it to sound dirty, and it did.

Totally gross. She made a moue of distaste. "If that is an example of your pickup lines, no wonder you have a hard time getting girls to go out on a date. Still, you kidnapped the wrong woman. You are not getting any of this." She gestured to her body, which drew his attention. Good, if he was staring at titties, then he wasn't paying attention to what she really had planned.

"You can't stop me from doing whatever I want with you."

"That's what you think. I don't see any drugs this time." No needles meant she had a fighting chance. She wouldn't underestimate his speed or strength this time. She had to fight smart against him. *And don't let him bite you.* The loss of motivation and control was not something she cared to repeat.

Her kidnapper sneered. "I won't need drugs to subdue you. I only use those when taking a pair. It's quieter that way. But two is too much work. All that flying back and forth to carry the bodies. Much easier to just steal one and really savor it. Although, I will miss the crying and the pleading. The women really didn't do well with my dining on their mates in front of them." He displayed sharp teeth.

He also displayed a villainous ego that enjoyed talking about himself. *Keep it up.* It gave Luna a chance to scout things out. 'Course, the only real choice was behind her. But she wasn't sure if the hall would lead to a possible escape or just pen her down in an even worse spot.

She'd never find out standing around in the buff. Bending down, she snared the edge of her blouse and managed to get an irritated, "What are you doing?"

"Getting dressed. Since you're taking your sweet time getting to the point, I'm getting chilly." And if she had to climb, she wanted a layer to protect her skin.

Fur is best. You'd never convince a feline otherwise.

"Put these on too." He flung her skirt at her. "You wouldn't want me to be distracted with you while in flight."

"I am not flying with you."

"We are leaving. Even now, Charlemagne is probably following. But he thinks I'm elsewhere. I played the role of servant and saboteur well."

"What the hell are you yapping about?" she asked, feeling a little more confidence now that her coochie—as Jeoff would say—wasn't hanging out.

"Stop talking and come here."

"Sorry, I've already got a guy friend, kind of, maybe." It was complicated.

"Come here. Now."

She took a step back and smirked. "Make me."

He stomped forward, and his foot went right through the flooring, trapping it.

It was the moment she'd hoped for. She bolted into the horror movie hallway, running for the dark shadow, recognizing the elevator shaft for what it was. A way down.

From behind, her kidnapper yelled as his dinner ran away.

Running. Snuffle. Her lioness expressed her dissatisfaction.

Sulk all you want. Luna preferred to live. Lionesses might be crazy, but they weren't stupid. They knew better than to take on odds that were against them. Bad odds were something best dealt with her crew.

And when she found her buds, they'd hunt down this bastard and show him what happened to those who hurt the pride.

If she escaped.

Chapter Sixteen

I can't fucking believe that asshole escaped.

The thought had Jeoff stomping back into the club in search of someone to blame. Unfortunately for him, the fight inside appeared to have ended with most of the players flat on the floor. No one left for him to hit. Fuck. Only a handful had been left standing, Charlemagne being one of them, as was Arik. Reba and the big bat dude also seemed unscathed, if glaring at each other.

The limp bodies nagged him. "Are they all dead?" He couldn't help an appalled note. He'd grown rather fond of the pride's females—even if they drove him nuts—and would hate to see them gone.

"Simply sleeping." Charlemagne waggled his fingers. "Sometimes, it's smarter to avoid a battle."

Avoid battle when Jeoff needed something to hit? "But I thought you said treason was punishable by death."

For a moment, the other man's eyes turned a deep black, and by black, Jeoff meant the entire orb. "Oh, they will be punished. Never fear. There are no second chances for whampyr who betray their master."

"So you'll punish these ones. Whoopedy-doo. What of the one who got away? Your mutiny leader is still out there, and we still don't know where Luna is."

"She is probably at his lair."

"Lair?" Arik repeated the word.

It was an odd word to use that evoked images of a dark cave and musty smells.

"Lair. Safe house. Whatever you wish to call it. The whampyr might be created to act as servants, but part of their nature is a need to keep themselves a lair of some sort, a hideout they can scuttle to should the need arise."

"A need for what?"

"That is not something you need to know." Charlemagne angled his head. "And while we discuss the whampyr habits, you are allowing him time to change locations. If we make haste, we should find him."

"You know where this hideout is?"

"Indeed. I am master in more than just name, wolf."

However, ten minutes later, standing at the base of the condemned building, Jeoff had to wonder if Charlemagne had fucked with him. Not a single scent trace in and around the area belonged to Luna. The various entrances to the building were boarded tight and showed no signs of tampering or entry.

"Are you sure they're in here?" Jeoff asked. Or was this Charlemagne's way of stalling them and allowing that monster to harm Luna?

"Such skepticism."

"Can you blame me?"

"Not a bit. You're right to be wary. It is, after all, in your nature. Animals always know when they encounter a predator."

"I should just kill you," Jeoff snarled, because surely Arik had a law against letting pompous asshats live.

"No killing," Arik grumbled as he climbed out

of his car, phone to his ear. "Apparently, he's got friends in high places, and they would be most displeased if something happened to him."

"Who the fuck told you what to do? You're king," Jeoff asked with a frown, only to almost immediately mutter an "oh" of understanding. Only one group had the power to order Arik. The High Council, a group of shifters never seen, and yet, from the shadows, they pulled and dangled the puppet strings that kept their civilization safe. Screwing with them meant disappearing in the night, all traces gone, and no one ever mentioning your name again. Or so the whispers said. No one ever spoke of those who disappeared.

"Now that I've been vouched for, then perhaps you might wish to hasten things along. The one you seek is within, but you need to stop wasting time. I don't think he's thinking too rationally. The girl might suffer if you linger."

Snarl. The mention of Luna in danger didn't sit well at all. It also didn't change the fact that the building was sealed shut. Jeoff traced the edges of the plywood barring his way and frowned. How to get in? Someone wanted to make sure no one entered, given the absurd number of nails used to affix it. "I don't suppose anyone has a crow bar?"

Apparently, the pride had quite a few in the trunks of their vehicles. Stacey handed him one, and Jeoff fitted it into the crack and pushed. The squeal of nails pulling free mixed with that of wood cracking and popping. From the small gap he created wafted an unbelievable stench.

Death.

Decay.

Delightful.

And his wolf wondered why Jeoff preferred to choose the cologne when he went shopping.

The olfactory evidence of violence didn't deter Jeoff or the others. In short order, torn plywood littered the ground and the miasma of decaying flesh permeated the air. With so many points of entry, they penetrated the lower level of the building, a sad reminder of the past.

Once, many decades ago, this place had served as an apartment complex built for low-income families. It was based on simple lines. Long hallway with doors off to either side. At one end there was an elevator, at the other, a stairway.

Which way should he go? Then again, given the lack of power, the choice seemed evident. Except…the stairs didn't reek, and Jeoff was working with curious cats who wanted to see what was in the elevator.

With that stench, Jeoff could almost guarantee it wouldn't be anything good. Even Hayder, a usually tough lion, blanched at the sight that met their eyes when they hauled the doors open.

No one could be unaffected by the pile of bodies dumped in the shaft, many of them in partially eaten states, ignobly piled atop the cab of the elevator permanently stopped one flow below. Their discovery explained the source of the reek. Of more concern, despite the damage, Jeoff recognized a body close to the top of the pile.

"That's the missing wolf pack member."

And Reba pointed out the missing tiger couple. As to the rest… Perhaps DNA and dental records would give their families closure.

A certain amount of relief imbued him as he noted no fresher corpses, more specifically, no Luna corpse. He might have gone nuts if he'd found it.

The faint sound of fighting came to them from up above. High above. The lionesses, some stripping for the second time that evening, went bolting for the stairs, a mini army of gold determined to reach the top of the tower.

But Jeoff noted the metal rungs embedded in the concrete shaft of the elevator. A straight shot up and possibly more solid than the other routes.

Before he could talk himself out of it, he tapped Leo on the shoulder. "I need you to vault me."

"Vault you where?" the big lion asked.

You had to love friends that didn't ask why. Jeoff pointed. "Over the bodies. I need to get to that ladder."

"Done."

In short order, with Leo's mighty boost, Jeoff was clambering up the rusted rungs, pushing himself, knowing that each second counted. The trek of several stories was long and, at times, frightening, especially when the grasp of one bar saw it pulling free from the wall. Jeoff dropped it, only to wince as he imagined it landing amidst the corpses.

So long as it's not me using them as a safety net.
Shudder.

He kept climbing, noting that, past the sound of his harsh pant of exertion, he could hear a struggle happening. A fight as Luna did her best to save herself.

He climbed faster and had just poked his head over the rim of the shaft when he noted a half-naked Luna streaking toward him, and, stalking behind her, the bat dude.

It gave him an idea. "Get on my back," he shouted, bracing himself against the rungs, hoping they would hold not just his, but now Luna's weight, as well.

"Are you treating me like a girl and saving me?" she yelled as she dropped to her haunches by the edge.

"Totally. It's what good boyfriends do."

"We're not dating." She peered over the edge.

"According to you. But, good news, I'm tenacious."

"I thought that was a characteristic of bull terriers."

"And wolves," he quipped, all the while keeping his eye on bat dude, who uttered a cry of rage as Luna wrapped her arms around him and lowered herself into the shaft. Her thighs nudged his hips, clamping onto him, but he still cautioned her to, "Hold on tight." Because the ride down could get bumpy.

Descents always proved much faster, especially since he could just toe the rung below and drop to it. From overhead the bat dude griped, "You won't get far. I'll find you. I have your taste now. You'll never escape me."

Jeoff saw no need to chastise Luna for loosening one arm long enough to flash her middle finger and utter a very eloquent, "Fuck you."

As antagonizing psycho creatures went, it worked rather well. The monster screamed, a wordless invective of sound, but more worrisome was it abruptly cut off. What did that mean? Had the lionesses made it to that top floor using the stairs?

Nope.

"He's following us," Luna muttered.

And, by follow, Luna didn't mean he used the ladder. The monster dropped down and grabbed at

Luna as he passed, tearing her from Jeoff's back.

"Luna!" He screamed her name, the darkness mocking him. He could see nothing looking down, only shadows.

He took the rungs at breakneck speed and almost missed the scent. There, on the third floor, through the partially opened elevator doors, Luna's scent clung to the edges. Jeoff thrust himself through that opening and caught a glimpse of the bat dude and Luna at the far end. Faint light illuminated the edges of the plywood covering the window to the outside, outlining them clearly.

Jeoff growled and ran, his rage mighty, mighty enough that he managed to drop some claws and his teeth elongated. A fierce primal anger thrummed through him.

The creature held Luna by his side, one-armed, much to her spitting irritation. The wham used its free hand to punch at the plywood covering the window. It splintered under his assault, revealing the outside.

He's gonna fly. Fuck no. If the bat dude escaped with Luna now, they might never find her again. Jeoff put on a burst of speed, determined to reach him before that happened. Just as the wham dragged Luna close, Luna reacted, sinking her teeth into its arm, biting hard enough to tear off a chunk. Uttering a cry of rage, the wham released her, dark blood pumping from his wound.

Luna spat. "Tastes like shit."

"Fucking whore!" the monster screamed. "You will pay for that."

For a moment, Jeoff thought he'd grab Luna again, but their eyes met, and the bat dude, instead, thrust its head and upper shoulders through the hole it made to the outside.

Perfect. Jeoff leaped the final few feet, his human legs bunching and coiling with bristling power. He extended his hands and caught at the monster's wings before he could push himself through the window.

The creature bellowed in rage as Jeoff held them and pulled, the disturbing sound of ripping fleshy paper and cracking bone distinctive.

The thrashing by the monster proved mighty and flung Jeoff hard enough that he hit the wall and partially sank into the soggy plaster. He pushed himself away and could only watch as the monster hesitated in front of the open window, probably wondering if he should fly, given his wings were a little bent.

And then it didn't matter. Luna, with a mighty shove, sent the beast through the open space.

She immediately peeked her head out. "Shit," she muttered. "He can still use those things."

Jeoff sprinted to her side, and they both peered out the window, noting the bat dude had extended his wings and sought to soar. He wobbled and wavered. The monster righted itself and rose higher and higher. Out of reach, getting away, and he might have flown off if other shadows, winged ones, hadn't suddenly converged from several directions.

The wounded bat dude might have stood a chance against a single shifter, or two, but against its own kind and whilst trying to stay aloft on damaged wings?

It was hard to track the action, but they all heard the shrill shriek of triumph, and they all saw the head that came plummeting down, mouth forever open in surprise. It hit the pavement and shattered into dust, followed a moment later by the body.

It's over. Luna was safe and the monster dead.

Chapter Seventeen

Not all of the monsters are dead. The realization pulled a growl from Luna as she tore herself from Jeoff's grasp the moment they hit the pavement outside. She dove at the bat dude standing behind Charlemagne.

What she couldn't understand was why no one else was trying to kill him too.

"Luna, I command you to stop right now." Arik's voice rang out loud and clear.

"What?" The mental screeching of brakes halted her feet, and she turned an incredulous glare on her leader. "Why?"

"Stop because you cannot kill Gaston Charlemagne or his servants."

She turned her head back and looked at the dude in the suit. "I'm pretty sure I can take him."

"Doesn't matter if you can or not. You're not allowed to kill him."

"What?" She couldn't stem the plaintive note. "Why can't I kill him?" Luna heard the order from her king and didn't want to obey. "He's in cahoots with those murderous flying mice."

"Mice?" A chuckle left the suave club owner. "That is quite the amusing comparison, don't you think, Jean Francois."

Jean Francois crossed his arms over his massive gray-furred chest. "Perhaps the female needs glasses."

"Perhaps squeaky toys shouldn't talk unless I'm biting them," Luna snapped. "Can someone tell me what the hell is going on? Why aren't we turning these guys into carrion scraps?" Arik explained because it turned out she'd missed out on a few crucial discoveries during her abduction.

In a nutshell, Charlemagne had come to town for a fresh start in a new city with his crew of whampyrs—although she preferred Hayder's wham appellation. One of the older whams went nuts. Started to eat folks and covered it up. Apparently, shifters were a delicacy to the winged mice folk. *Blood is like wine.* They drank it usually from a cup unless they went old-school and took it from the vein like the dead dude did.

While no one had said it yet, Luna knew, as soon as they returned to the condo, the rumors would start of the vampires that had come to town. Vampires they were forbidden from killing. How could they allow them to stay? How come they didn't sharpen their claws and remove them from this world?

They are predators like us.

No, not like us. The lions killed to feed and protect.

Exactly.

Explain then the bodies in the shaft. Except Charlemagne did have an explanation. Basically, his servant had gone nuts. Apparently, it happened with the older ones of their kind, and he'd missed the signs. But the crazy mouse dude and those he'd converted were dead now. Yet, what of the rest? What of the club and its owner and those still alive by his side?

With a theatrical roll of his eyes, and a sigh of, "The things I do to keep the wildlife happy,"

Charlemagne agreed to abide by Arik's city rules out of courtesy, and Luna wondered how long this uneasy truce would last.

As the people who'd come to her rescue piled into vehicles and made plans to go find a place that served breakfast at four a.m., Charlemagne flicked dust from his lapels. "Now that we are done, if you'll excuse me, I have to make arrangements to hire new staff. Human staff, I think this time."

As the club owner turned to walk away, Arik growled. "We're not done. I still have questions."

"I'm sure you do, and I might decide to answer them. Eventually."

"You will—" There was no point in Arik finishing his sentence; Charlemagne was gone. Vanished into thin air.

"Fuck me, how does he do that?" Because Luna didn't believe in magic.

And apparently, Jeoff believed in miracles because she didn't know how he thought he wouldn't die when he announced, "Hayder, I'm going to borrow your wheels and take Luna back to my place."

"Oooh, someone is going to get lucky," Stacey sang.

"Do you have enough peanut butter?" snickered another of her crew. Luna, the has-no-shame-Luna of the pride, almost blushed as she recalled a conversation one night at the bar about how the only way to get a man to lick a pussy right was to put peanut butter on it and make sure you used a wolf.

"I don't have any clothes at your place," she argued.

"Awesome."

"Or a toothbrush."

"I have a spare somewhere, I'm sure."

"I thought I said no more getting involved."

"Don't make me cluck in front of your friends."

Luna noted the sly ladies of her crew eyeballing her and Jeoff. Eyeballing her man.

Not mine. But he could be.

Stacey strutted close, wearing some loose frock that delineated her braless state. Luna felt their close friendship might be coming to an end.

"If Luna doesn't want to go back with you, I'll come." Stacey winked.

Luna lost it. Only Jeoff's arms wrapped around her kept Luna from going after Stacey, who skipped out of reach with a giggle. "I knew she liked him. Luna likes Jeoff."

And that was what started "Luna and Jeoff sitting in a tree, Frenching naked as can be." The lyrics got dirtier from there, and Luna's cheeks got brighter as Jeoff hauled her off. What embarrassed her wasn't the song or even Jeoff's very intriguing manhandling. The thing that ripened her cheeks was it was true. She did like Jeoff.

And it scared the hell out of her.

Since when, though, did she let fear dictate her actions? She saw a high mountain; she climbed it. She saw a cookie jar on top of the fridge; she filched from it. She lusted after a six-footish wolf who seemed determined to become someone important in her life, and she should damn well let him fuck her as many times as he could manage. Because she was not afraid.

But what of tomorrow? What happens then?

She did an about-turn in the hall, only steps from his door, the loose track pants she'd managed to score for the ride over slipping over her ass as she practically jogged back to the elevator.

Jeoff easily caught her, and since she was apparently still under the influence of drugs, she let him carry her back to his place.

"We shouldn't be doing this. I don't know if I'm ready for commitment."

"So don't commit. Just do me."

"Do me?" She stopped wiggling on his shoulder, not too hard because, apparently, she wanted to be caught. "Is that supposed to be sexy?"

"I'd think it was sexy if you said it. Hell, I thought it was sexy just the way you repeated it. And, for your information, yes, I'd do you."

When a man said that to a woman, how could she help melting? Some might balk at the stark crudeness of it, but Luna saw to the core of it. The unvarnished truth. Jeoff wanted her.

She wanted him, and that was why she let him strip her, loving the slow drag of his fingers over her skin as he tugged it free of the fabric concealing it. She couldn't wait to feel the burning touch of his hands, palm pressed to her skin.

Instead of branding her, he led her to the bathroom. The shower water didn't take long to become warm, and he got in first, still holding her hand, then tugged her in.

Since speaking would probably ruin the moment, Luna kept quiet. Dirty talk had a time and place. But some moments, some intimate moments, where choices swung over a precipice, those needed no words. Soft touches, intense looks, the burning kiss by lips that devoured.

Jeoff uttered a soft growl when she nipped his lower lip then sucked it.

"You drive me wild." The words rumbled and shivered against her wet lips.

"Ditto, and not because you have an incontinence problem when you drink." She laughed, especially when his hands gripped her bare ass cheeks and yanked her close.

"That is the last time you'll ever compare me to anyone else. Because there will be no one else. Just me. And you."

He pinned her with words, and she fought the panicked flutter. Jeoff wanted to possess her.

Just like we shall own him. Remember, a monogamous relationship went two ways. By him claiming her, she could claim him, and no one else would touch.

No touch. No share. No one but her allowed to touch the skin she ran her fingers over, the shiver that went through his frame a heady thing.

"I am going to fuck you," he said as his hands left the curve of her buttocks to span her waist.

Her breath caught at his words. So filthy. And from Jeoff. "Maybe I'll fuck you first." She did so like to ride on top.

He spun her and leaned against her back, pressing her into the cold tile. "It's okay to let go. To let someone else be in charge."

"I don't have power issues." She shoved against him, only to have him cage her between his arms, his body tucked behind, the evidence of his erection pointing upward and pressed against the crevice of her buttocks. Decadently hot.

She almost missed his next words as she held her breath in anticipation, waiting for his next touch.

"I am going to take you, Luna. I am going to take you. Not just once, not twice, but as many times as it takes until you realize I'm here to stay."

"That could take a while."

"I know. Which just proves my point."

"Can't you prove your point another way?" She wiggled her ass against him, causing him to lean down and nip at her ear.

Her breath caught. How she loved a good ear nibble. She melted into a puddle against him as his lips and tongue explored the shell and lobe of her ear. She rotated against him, her breathing coming in hot pants, her fingers scrabbling at the tile wall.

The hands at her waist spun her around to face him again, and he raised her with ease. His hard lips met hers in a fiery kiss that stole her breath but ignited every single nerve ending. The cold tile wall pressed against her back when he propped her against it, a stark counter to her burning skin.

Speaking of skin, his touched hers in many spots, and she didn't want to lose it, so she drew him closer with arms wrapped around his neck while her legs locked around his waist.

Their lips slid and caressed in wet abandon. His tongue slipped into her mouth, and she returned the favor. His grumble of pleasure caused shivers to erupt. Mouths meshed intimately and left his hands free to roam from her waist to the underside of her thighs. It allowed him to manhandle her until his cock bobbed just under her sex.

The head of his prick stroked at her sex, parting her swollen nether lips, pressing into her. She couldn't help but throw her head back, gasping for air, trying to make a sound as he penetrated her, this second time possibly better than the first. He sheathed himself in her, a long molten steel rod, and she clutched at his shoulders.

He began to move, his hips rotating, slow, circular pushing. Deep inside. She tightened.

A slight withdrawal and then a hard thrust. Gasp and an even tighter fist around his cock.

Over and over, he teased her, claimed her until she begged for relief.

"Please. Oh, yes."

He swallowed her words. "Come for me," he whispered.

Yes. Yes. YES!

His fingers dug into her thighs, maintaining his grip as he slammed his shaft deep in her channel. Over and over and over again. She reached the point of no sound, her body taut and ready to snap. Harder he pistoned, slamming in and out of her channel, the slick friction enough to shove her over the edge. And bring him with her.

They did eventually fall into bed, a naked pile of limbs that she totally enjoyed, even if he did ruin it by saying, "This is nice."

"Nice is for pussies."

"Guess we're okay then."

"Just because I slept with you again doesn't make us a couple."

"If you say so."

"I mean it."

"I know."

"Wanna fuck again?"

Hell yeah, she did. They could talk about the fact this was just a two-time thing in the morning.

Epilogue

A few months later…

The warm rays of the sunshine were blocked by a shadow. She opened one eye to see her body covered by Jeoff, his forearms stretched to hold him hovering above, his naked lower body pressing in a most interesting fashion.

"You're blocking my sunshine, wolfie." Although the heat radiating from his expression more than made up for it.

"About time you woke up. Thought we might do a little something-something before I went to work." He made his meaning clear with a thrust of his hips.

How far he'd come in the time they'd spent together, openly admitting his lust for her in the most delightful ways. She also lusted, so it worked. They helped each other scratch an itch. She expected it would end any day now.

Snort. Okay, even she didn't believe that one anymore.

She wiggled against his erection, loving how his eyes flared in reply. "Are you sure you have time? You might be late. Or maybe this is just an urge to pee."

"This isn't a need to pee. I already did that out on the balcony."

"You what?"

"Marked your balcony."

"What for?"

He rolled his eyes. "Because I'm a guy and we pee on things."

"But you're not drunk. My ex only did that when he was wasted."

A smile pulled his lips. "So I heard, which is why you'll either have to get rid of the chair in the living room, let me pee on it, or move in with me."

The easy reply was to rid herself of the offensive chair. But she was too shocked by his demand for commitment. "And why should I move in with you? Why wouldn't you move in with me? I've got a perfectly nice place for us to share."

"Okay."

She blinked. "Okay?"

"Yes, I'll move in with you. Is that formal enough?"

"Are you serious? You really want to move in?"

"A little slow this morning, are we?"

"Just making sure."

He grinned. "Very sure. Just like I'm very sure what day it is today."

"What day is that?" She wrinkled her nose. Christmas had passed. As had New Year's. She was pretty sure his birthday was in the summer. What did that leave? "Holy shit, did I forget to get you something pretty for Valentine's?"

He sighed.

"Oh, would you stop it already and spit it out? What did I forget?"

"Remember how you once said you'd never made it past the three-month mark with a guy?"

"Yeah." She remembered. "Is this your way to

taunting me with the fact we made it to four?"

"You knew!"

"Of course I did. But if you ask me, it's not that big of a deal."

"Says the woman scared of commitment."

"Don't start, wolfie. I recall someone who wasn't too keen on hitting it with a lioness."

"I was wrong. I can admit it."

"Just like I can admit maybe this wasn't such a bad idea."

"I love you too." He said it without the least sarcasm, and she frowned at him.

"Just because we're still together doesn't mean we need to make a big deal out of it. I mean, you and me, this thing we have, maybe it was kind of meant to be. I…" She took in a deep breath. She could do this. It was just three little words. "I love you."

"Finally she admits it." His eyes shone. "About time."

"Don't expect me to admit it in public. I wouldn't want to ruin my street cred with the crew."

"Too late." He held up his smart phone. "I got it on video."

Her gaze narrowed. "Give that back."

"Make me."

She did. Naked. Then uploaded it herself because it seemed only fair to give the biatches yet another warning that Jeoff was taken. Paws off or face the claw. *Snarl*.

*

The stiletto tips of her swanky heels clacked and Reba's ample hips swung as she strutted past the line waiting to get through the door. Lines were for sheep. And this lioness wasn't about to wait her turn.

Ignoring the protests of those not graced with awesomeness, she placed herself ahead of them, only to find her entrance blocked.

Lacking a certain height advantage didn't mean Reba didn't peer upward and grace the bouncer with a look. *The look.* The kind that said, "Move your ass, bubba." In this case, bubba was a big ol' human, and he was silly enough to hold a hand up, blocking her path.

"You can't go in there."

"I'm expected," she announced.

"No one told me nothing about no special guests, so get to the back of the line."

Was this human seriously getting in her way? Viper quick, she reached out, grabbed his wrist, and yanked him close, close enough for him to see the primal amber of her beast glowing in her eyes. "Don't get in my way. I've made bigger men cry."

A sharp twist of the hand and bubba hit the ground, his round face blanched in pain. She did so forget her own strength sometimes when dealing with the sheep.

Arik said to not call them that.

Arik also said they shouldn't pounce on the pizza delivery boy until he squeaked. As if she and the crew listened. It was part of their Friday night ritual.

Spotting the earpiece the bouncer wore, she leaned close and whispered, "Ready or not, here I come," before releasing the human. He rocked back on his haunches and shot her a sullen glare, but he didn't try to stop her as she stepped inside. She found herself in an outer chamber with benches lining the walls and another door. A pair of gaudily dressed females—more humans—gaped at her. They hugged clipboards to their chests. They also wore earpieces. Reba blew them a kiss and laughed as they recoiled.

What was it about her appearance that made them so leery of her? Who cared? She strode to the second set of doors. Upon opening them, she noted more staff dressed in black T-shirts converging on her.

At least they showed enough respect to send more than one. A lady liked to think she was appreciated. Before she could make them sing soprano, they halted, rather abruptly, and turned around, melting back into the shadows they used to hide. Probably because a certain stealthy guy stood behind her.

"Couldn't you have waited a few more minutes? I was hoping for some exercise," she complained.

"If I'd known you were coming, I'd have had my staff lay out a path of rose petals and greeted you myself at the door," said a voice that belonged on late night radio, saying dirty things when she was alone in bed with her battery operated friend.

"Why waste time?" Reba announced. Arik had given her a job to do and no time like the present to handle it.

Pivoting on her heel, she took in the svelte appearance of Gaston Charlemagne, and just like the first time she'd met him, she had to wonder what the hell everyone was talking about when they said he had no scent. He smelled perfectly fine to her. More than fine. Decadent chocolate with a hint of smoky mystery. The aroma made her taste buds water.

Wanna take a bite.

"Go ahead." He bared his throat. "Have a nibble."

The invitation was less freaky than the fact

that—*HE READ MY FUCKING MIND!*

The End…until Reba returns in *When A Lioness Pounces*

Author Bio

Hello and thank you so much for reading my story. I  hope I kept you well entertained. As you might have noticed, I enjoy blending humor in to my romance. If you like my style then I have many other wicked stories that might intrigue you so please visit EveLanglais.com

Facebook: http://bit.ly/faceevel
Twitter: @evelanglais
Newsletter: http://evelanglais.com/newrelease